Mason

Catalogue of the Smith cabinet

Part first. 10/05/1880

Mason

Catalogue of the Smith cabinet
Part first. 10/05/1880

ISBN/EAN: 9783741197666

Manufactured in Europe, USA, Canada, Australia, Japa

Cover: Foto ©Andreas Hilbeck / pixelio.de

Manufactured and distributed by brebook publishing software
(www.brebook.com)

Mason

Catalogue of the Smith cabinet

CATALOGUE

—OF—

❦THE ✠ SMITH ✠ CABINET❧

[PART FIRST.]

Comprising a large and varied assortment of American and Foreign Gold,
Silver, Copper, Bronze and Nickel Coins, Medals, &c., also, Ancient
Greek and Roman Gold, Silver and Bronze Coins and
Medals; Paper Money, Numismatic Books,
and a large assortment of Store Cards,
Politicals in Silver and Copper,
Personals, &c., &c.

Included in the two sales will be found the U. S. Silver Dollars of
1794, 1836, 1838, 1839, 1851, 1852 and '58.

ALL THE RARE U. S. HALF DOLLARS; ALL BUT TWO OF THE
U. S. QUARTERS; ALL THE U. S. DIMES; ALL THE U. S.
HALF DIMES; MANY FINE AND UNCIRCULATED U S
CENTS, HALF CENTS, AND A LARGE VARIETY OF AMER-
ICAN COLONIAL COINS.

A portion of the above will be offered at each days Sale.

BANGS & CO., Auctioneers,

739 & 741 BROADWAY, NEW YORK.

Tuesday, Wednesday and Thursday. October 5, 6, 7, 1880.

Commencing each Day at 2.30 o'clock,

Catalogued by MASON & CO.

143 NORTH TENTH STREET, PHILADELPHIA.

☞The Auctioners will execute any Bids entrusted to them.☜

PRESS OF
EDWARD HIRSCH & CO., 30 South Fourth St,
PHILADELPHIA.

EXPLANATORY.

The owner of the Smith Cabinet, fearing that a six days continuous coin sale would prove tedious and otherwise inconvenient to many buyers, concluded to divide his extensive collection, and make at proper intervals two sales of three days each ; and in adopting this plan, we would state, that our object has been to give as varied a character to each sale as possible ; hence we have selected for each day a good portion of the choice pieces in each series to interlard the great quantity and variety of those pieces not generally so highly valued. In pursuing the above course, we have sacrificed, in a measure, system to convenience. A package of catalogues of Part 1, has been expressed to each Coin Dealer in the U. S. and Canada, and a large number of single copies mailed to Collectors, whose names are upon our books to date. In case any dealer should require a further supply of catalogues, or if any omissions have occured, immediate notice to the undersigned will supply the deficiency. All coins, medals, &c., in both sales, are guaranteed genuine, unless otherwise described. Attention is solicited to the grand opportunity, afforded by the two sales, to secure bargains among the lots offered in various portions of the catalogue. Collectors of foreign silver and copper coins, medals, &c., will find much of interest under these headings, while collectors of Business Cards, Politicals, American Medals, &c., will find a rich field to help out their series. The rare and fine American pieces in the catalogues speak for themselves, and a number will command unusual attention for rarity and condition. Catalogues of Part II will be distributed early in September, the sale to occur October 19, 20, 21. Early notice is desired from Coin Dealers of the number of catalogues required. Vol. II, No. 2, of our *Coin Collectors' Herald*, (out in Aug.) will contain some particulars of the Second Sale.

MASON & CO.,

143 North Tenth Street,

Phila., August, 1880.   PHILADELPHIA.

CATALOGUE.

MISCELLANEOUS COINS, MEDALS, PAPER MONEY, &C.

1 1877 Two admission tickets to Capitol at the counting of vote for President and Vice. Signed T. W. Ferry and Sam Randall. February 19th, 1877.

2 Six C. S. A. brass Army and Navy buttons, various.

3 1773 Rhode Island Colonial Note, fifteen shillings, clean.

4 Three C. S. A. bonds, signed, with coupons.

5 Two $100.00 C. S. A. interest notes, rare.

6 One $500.00 C. S. A. note, Richmond, scarce.

7 Five $100.00 C. S. A. notes. Blue backs.

8 Five $50.00 "   "   "   "

9 Five $20.00 "   "   "   "

10 Five $10.00 "   "   "   "

11 Five $5 00 "   "   "   "

12 Fifty C. S. A. notes 5 cts. to $1.00, varieties.

13 Six $100.00 bonds C. S. A. Coupons signed.

14 Four President Johnson Impeachment tickets, varieties.

15 1851 London Exhibition, (W. Metal Medal), size 32. Proof.

16 Henry I, English copper medal, fine, size 21. Rare.

17 Washington Medal, "Ugly Head," copper, proof, size 22.

18 "   "   "   "   brass,   "   "   "

19 Forty large and small Foreign copper coins, tokens, &c. Good.

20 1854 Gold plated Canadian coin badge, fine.

21 Two U. S. Dimes, 1805 and 1807, poor.

22 Treason copper token, Canada, fine, rare.

23 Three fine copies, 1793 and '96 half cents and 1809 cent.

24 Silver and copper Chinese coins, size of dime, fine, 2 pieces.

25 Eight copper and brass political medalets, fine, rare.

26 Twelve uncirculated store cards, brass, copper and w. metal.

27 1783 Two brass Washington coins, fair. (Unity.)

28 1829 Magnificent Wellington Medal, " Ireland pacified." Bronze proof, size 36, rare.

29 Brass Washington piece "Success to the U. S." uncirculated, rare.
30 1850 and 1853 U. S. Cents, bright, uncirculated, 2 pieces:
31 Colonel James Fisk, brass medalet, Chicago, fine, rare.
32 Two Idler's copies Lord Baltimore penny, copper and nickel, uncirculated.
33 1823 Cassini medal, bronze, proof, size 26.
34 Milan Cathedral medal, in bas relief, thick bronze, size 20, proof.
35 1855 U. S. silver three cent piece, good, scarce.
36 1872, '73 California gold half and quarter, pierced, 2 pieces
37 1872, '75   "   "   "   "   "   "
38 1876   "   "   " fine.
39 U. S. Dime, a curiosity, resembles 1799, very poor.
40 1822 U. S. Dime, extremely poor.
41 Eight small Foreign silver and base coins, various, fair.
42 Twenty-six Colonials, Conn., N. J. &c., poor to good.
43 1773 Four Virginia cents, fair to good.
44 One Japanese ¼ Bou, gold, intrinsic value $1.00, fine.
45 1801 U. S. dime, pierced, poor, date shows.
46 1809   "   " very fair, scarce.
47 1814   "   " small date, good.
48 1820 '3 "   " good, 2 pieces.
49 1870 '1 Jamaica Coins, nickel, good, scarce, 2 pieces.
50 1799 three 1799 U. S. cents, altered. Fair.
51 1792 Coventry half penny, nude figure, good, scarce.
52 Four small base Haytian coins, fine.
53 Nine English Tokens, &c., good to fine.
54 1792 Solid copper Washington cent, copy, fine.
55 1792 Lead copy   "   " poor.
56 1791 Brass cast, Washington cent, poor.
57 1799 U. S. cent, very poor.
58 1821 Gilmor marriage medal. Obverse 2 busts; reverse Cupid in bas relief, bronze, proof, rare, size 36.
59 Admission ticket of Electoral Commission.

SMALL AMERICAN STORE CARDS,
1861 TO '64.

The following Collection of Store Cards embraces a number of rare types and varieties. An examination of these pieces, now becoming scarce, will result in advantage to buyer.

60 1864 R. S. Torry, "Bee Hive," Bangor, Me., copper, fine.
61 1863 Charnley, [Anchor,] Providence, R. I. copper, fine.
62 1863   "   " variety, "   "

63 A. W. Wallace, Baker, Bridgeport, R. I. copper, fine.
64 Weller's News Depot, Norwich, R. I.   "   "
65 1861 to '64 A collection of store cards from various cities and towns in the state of N. Y. in good to uncirculated condition, some very rare, 89 copper and 9 brass varieties, 98 pieces.
66 1863 Neptune House, Atlantic City, N. J., copper, good, 2 pieces.
67 Warrick & Stanger, Glassboro, N. J. brass, fine.
68 1863 J. Wightman, Newark, N. J. copper, uncirculated.
69 B. W. Titus, Trenton, N. J. brass, fine.
70 1861 to '64 A collection of 31 copper and 10 brass Store cards from various cities and towns, good to uncirculated, many scarce, 41 pieces.
71 A set of cards bearing Head of Liberty obv. Reverses, Clarridge & Co., Baltimore, Md. Schriver & Co. Union Mills, Md. Dorman's, Baltimore, Md. brass, fine, 3 pieces.
72 A lot (all different,) copper and brass cards, Baltimore, Md. fine, 7 pieces.
72½ Barry & M'Donnel, Soda, Knoxville, Tenn. brass, fine.
73 1863 Eckhart, Hosiery, Wheeling, W. Va. copper, fine.
74 Feibelmans, Saloon, Petersburg, Va. brass, fine.
75 1863 Jenkens, Clothier, St. Louis, Mo. copper, fine.
76 1861 Peck, Grocer, Chicago, Ill. copper, good.
77 1861 Childs Mauer, Die Sinker, Chicago, Ill. copper, good.
78 1863 Slade, Grain, Rockford, Ill. copper, poor.
79 1863 Dean & Slade, Dry Goods, Palatine, Ill. copper, fair.
80 Lininger & Bro. Dry Goods, Peru, Ill. copper, good.
81 1863 Queeby, Peru, Ind. [2]; M'Creery; Boston Store; Geisendoref & Co. Roll & Smith, Indianapolis, Ind. Allegre & Wroughton, Albany, Ind. Baldwin, Greensboro, Ind. Green & Co., Elkhart, Ind. Rowe, Corunna, Ind. March, Goshen, Ind. Pottenger & Co., Warsaw, Ind. Copper, fine, 12 pieces
82 1861, '3 Collection of fine and good cards, 68 copper, 3 brass, all different, 71 pieces. Ohio.
83 1861, '3 Collection of fine and good cards, 36 copper, 2 brass, all different, 38 pieces. Ohio.
84 1863 Collection of fine cards, all different, copper, 11 pieces. Ohio.
85 1875 Dittrich, Hatter, D. C. all different, brass. fine, 3 pcs.
86 Hurdle, Patents, Washington, D. C. brass, fine.
87 Union Club, Washington, D. C. brass, fine.

AMERICAN WAR TOKENS, 1861 '2.

88 A fine collection of different war tokens, selected with care, large number scarce and some rare, all in fine to uncirculated condition. No dates. Size of small store cards. 204 copper, 8 brass, 2 lead, 214 pieces.

SUTLERS' CARDS. &C.

89 A collection of Sutlers' cards, soda water, and other tokens without date, 55 brass, 8 copper, 4 nickel, all different, good to fine, 67 pieces.

SPIEL MARKS.

90 A collection of brass Spiel Marks or game tokens, large and small, fine, 50 pieces.
91 Yankee Robinson, circus, 5 copper, 1 tin, all different, fine, 6 pieces.
92 Brooks, Canton can works, silver, fine, scarce.

MEDIUM SIZE STORE CARDS.

93 Copper and brass store cards, between old Half Cent and Cent size, interesting collection of varieties from various states, 105 pieces.
94 Collection of large and small Foreign Jetons, brass, fine, 108 pieces.
95 Ten, five and one cent U. S. Stamps, enclosed in frames, used for change, fine, brass, 3 pieces.

POLITICAL TOKENS, 1837 TO 41., &C.

96 Collection of Political Tokens, all different, uncirculated, copper, some rare, size of old cent, 24 pieces.
97 Same, different varieties from last, good, 6 pieces.
98 Collection of 1837 large copper Store Cards, of same character as the political tokens in appearance, some rare, copper, good to uncirculated, 41 pieces.
99 Collection of large brass Am. Store Cards, size of old copper cent, fine to uncirculated. An excellent lot of varieties, (period 1837 to '41,) 40 pieces.
100 Collection of large Copper Am. Store Cards, size of copper cent, fine to uncirculated, period 1837 to '41, 40 pieces.

ENGLISH COPPER TOKENS.

101　25 Penny Tokens, large and thick, good to fine, all different.
102　25 Penny Tokens, large and thick, good to fine, all different.
103　25 Half Penny Tokens, uncirculated, all different.
104　25　"　　"　　"　　　"　　　.　　"　　"
105　25　"　　"　　"　　　"　　　　　"　　"
106　25　"　　"　　"　　　"　　　　　"　　"
107　4　"　　"　　"　　proofs　　　"　　"　　scarce.
108　25　"　　"　　".　good to v. fine,　"　　"
109　25　"　　"　　"　　"　　"　　"　　"　　"
110　25　"　　"　　"　　good to fine,　　"　　"
111　25　"　　"　　"　　"　　"　　"　　"
112　25　"　　"　　"　　"　　"　　"　　"
113　39　"　　"　　"　　"　　"　　"　　"
114　1792 Lady Godiva ½ Penny, good, scarce.
115　1794　"　　"　　"　　"　　"
116　A collection of small English tokens, size of U. S. Half
　　　Cent, good to fine, 68 pieces.
(The above lots 101 to 116 inc. form a collection of different types and varieties, and would make an interesting and fine lot for a buyer interested in the historical incidents, manufactures, &c., of England, during a period of scarcity of coins for small change, at the latter part of the 18th Century, all original.)

CALIFORNIA GOLD COINS, &C.

117　1854 Gold Dollar.　Oct.　Uncirculated.　Scarce
118　1874　"　　"　　"　　Proof　　　"
119　1864 Gold Half Dollar.　Oct.　Proof.　Scarce.
120　1871　"　　"　　"　　"　　"　　"
121　1873　"　　"　　"　　"　　"　　"
122　1874　"　　"　　"　　"　　"　　"
123　1875　"　　"　　"　　"　　"　　"
124　1876　"　　"　　"　　"　　"　　"
125　1852　"　　"　　"　　Round.　Unc.　"
126　1852　"　　"　　"　　"　　"　variety, scarce.
127　1867　"　　"　　"　　"　　"　Scarce.
128　1871　"　　"　　"　　"　　"　　"
129　1874　"　　"　　"　　"　　"　　"
130　1875　"　　"　　"　　"　　"　　"
131　1876　"　　"　　"　　"　　"　　"
132　1866 Gold Quarter Dollar.　Oct.　Unc.　Scarce.

133   1868 Gold Quarter Dollar.   Oct.   Unc.   Scarce.
134   1871   "   "   "   "   "   "
135   1873   "   "   "   "   "   "
136   1874   "   "   "   "   "   "
137   1875   "   "   "   "   "   "
138   1876   "   "   "   "   "   "
139   no date "   "   "   Round   "   Rare.
140   1864   "   "   "   "   "   Scarce.
141   1870   "   "   "   "   "   "
142   1870   "   "   "   "   "   variety, scarce.
143   1871   "   "   "   "   "   Scarce.
144   1873   "   "   "   "   "   "
145   1874   "   "   "   "   "   "
146   1875   "   "   "   "   "   "
147   1858 U S. Quarter Eagle, brass copy, uncirculated.
148   1858   "   "   "   "   fine.
149   1853, '4, '6 and '7 U. S Dollars, brass and lead copies, good, 7 pieces.
150   "Texas Dollar." A silver planchet, dollar size, with a countersunk shield bearing a "lone star" centre of obverse, 1. P. in lower margin ; reverse, blank, fine, rare.

ANCIENT GREEK SILVER COINS, &C.

151   Drachma of Athens.   Owl and Olive, fair, rare.
152   Hemidrachm   "   Owl facing, fair, rare.
153   Diabolus   "   Owl, good, rare.
154   Drachma of Argos.   Forepart of a Wolf, good, rare.
155   "   "   Rotona.   A dove, rare.
156   "   "   Licyon.   Chimara and Dove, fine, rare
157   Hemidrachm   "   Two doves, fair rare.
158   Two Drachma, uncertain.   Both good.   "   2
159   Drachma of Philip II, good but bored.   "
160   Plated lead cast of Drachma of Alexander the Great.
161   Small bronze of Messenia Tripod, fair, scarce.
162   Copper of Pharnaces, small size, very fine, scarce.
163   Ten small bronze, Greek.   Poor to fair.   10

ANCIENT ROMAN COINS.

SILVER DENARII.

161   Two Consular Denarii.   Fair, but misstruck.   2
165   Tiberius.   Tribute Penny.   Fair, interesting.
166   Three of Trajan.   Different reverses.   2 good, 1 broken.   3
167   Two of Hadrian.   "   "   Good.   2

168 Marcus Aurelius. Fine.
169 Caracalla. Happiness personified, very good.
170 Two of Gordian III. Different, base, good.
171 Tacitus Health personified, base, good, scarce.
172 Probus. Health personified, copper, good.
173 Six plated lead castings of Roman Denarii. Three con-
     sular and three imperial.   6

FIRST BRONZE.

174 Julius Cæsar. Pontifical implements, fine, false.
175 Caligula. Three men in a temple. Emperor seated in
     the Character of Piety. Poor, rare.
176 Agrippina Carpentum. Poor, rare.
177 Hadrian Justice. Poor.
178 Faustina Sr. Empress Sacrificing. Fair.
179 Julia Maxima. Happiness. Very poor.
180 Gordian II. Good Portrait. Poor.
181 Justinus. Pierced and very poor.
182 Twelve pieces of first Bronze. Poor.   12

SECOND BRONZE.

183 Caligula. Vesta. Fair, scarce.
184 Germanicus. Titles. Fair. "
185 Claudius. Liberty standing. Fair, scarce.
186 Nero. A victory. Fair, scarce.
187 Diocletian. Justice. Fair "
188 Maximian. Genius of Roman people. Very fine.
189 Constantius Chlorus. Justice. Very good.
190 Two Byzantine. Poor.   2
191 Lot of Second Bronze. 12 pieces. Poor.
192 Aurelian and Probus, third bronze, good.   2
193 Albetus. Third bronze. Poor, very rare.
194 Lot of third bronze. Fair to poor. 44 pieces.
195 Two bronze of Nero, one of Probus, Mint of Alexandria,
     very good. 3 pieces.

UNITED STATES PROOF SETS.

196 1858 Brilliant Proof Set. 7 p's. Very rare.
197 1862   "   "   "   "   Scarce.
198 1870   "   "   "   10 p's.   "
199 1871   "   "   "   "   "
200 1872   "   "   "   "   "
201 1873   "   "   "   Old style, 11 p's.,
     both Dollars, rare.

202 1873 Brilliant Proof Set.   Trade, 9 p's.   Rare.
203 1874   "   "   "   7 p's.
204 1875   "   "   "   8 p's.
205 1876   "   "   "   8 p's.   Scarce.
206 1877   "   "   "   8 p's., includes 20c.
     Very rare.
207 1879 Brilliant Proof Set.   7 p's.   Scarce.

AMERICAN AND FOREIGN MEDALS, MEDALETS, &c.

Size by American Scale in $\frac{1}{16}$ of an inch.

208 Medal cut out of solid Silver and elaborately engraved
     and chased obverse and reverse with ornamental open
     work, [swivel at top,] one eighth of an inch thick,
     weighs 4 silver dollars. Inscribed "Awarded to the
     Edna Quartette, by the Oneida Assembly for best
     singing, Jan. 19, 1875." Very fine.
209 Copy of the Celebrated Waterloo bronze proof Medal.
     Obverse in centre Busts of the four Georges, surround-
     ed by chariots, &c. Reverse emblematical nude
     figures in every variety of posture. The original of
     this Medal is in the British Museum, and copies are
     very rare, this cost $20. Size 5 inches in dia.
210 American Institute N. Y. Obverse Fame, Eagle, Shield,
     &c. Reverse awarded to Nathaniel Rider, 1845,
     intrinsic value $2.25, silver proof in velvet case,
     size 32.
211 Phila. Cathedral, white metal, in velvet case, fine, scarce.
     Size 52.
212 Ditto, bronze proof, rare.
213 Washington before Boston, bronze, pierced, original some-
     what abused, rare, size 42.
214 James Buchanan to Dr. Rose, bronze proof, thick,
     size 48, scarce
215 Thomas Jefferson, Indian Peace Medal, copy, size 40.
216 Washington before Boston, fine electrotype, size 42.
217 Obverse Oxford Cathedral, reverse Cathedral Choir,
     magnificent bronze proof, rare, size 38.
218 N. H. Agri. Soc., reverse, awarded to Mewell Hayes, in
     1872 for Baby Tender, bronze proof, size 38.
219 Obverse, bust of Major General Porter, reverse, Resolu-
     tion of Congress for battles of Chippewa, &c., bronze
     proof, size 40.

AMERICAN GOLD COINS.

220 1853 California Double Eagle, obverse, Eagle and Shield Legend "United States of America, Twenty Dollars, 900 Thous." Reverse, inscription in label, centre of fine lathe work, "United States Assay Office of Gold, San Francisco, Cal., 1853." Very fine, rare.

221 1795 U. S. Eagle. Uncirculated, rare.

222 1799 "   "   Very fine   "

223 1801 "   "   "   "   scarce.

224 1803 "   "   "   "   "

225 1798 United States Half Eagle, large Eagle, fine, scarce

226 1800   "   "   "   "   Very fine.

227 1802 over '01 U. S. Half Eagle,   "   "

228 1806 U. S. Half Eagle, fine.

229 1807 "   "   "   old style, head right. V. good.

230 1807 "   "   "   new style, head left. Unc.

231 1808 "   "   "   uncirculated.

232 1809 "   "   "   very fine.

233 1810 "   "   "   "   "

234 1811 "   "   "   uncirculated.

235 1804 U. S. Quarter Eagle, very fine, rare.

236 1849 U. S. Gold Dollar, (first Gold Dollar struck at the Phila. Mint,) uncirculated, rare.

237 "Rutherf: Bechtler, $2½," piece, reverse "*Carolina Gold*, 67 *grains*, 21 *carats*, uncirculated, very rare.

238 "Rutherf: Bechtler, $1," reverse, "Carolina Dollar, 28 grains", fine, rare.

239 "Rutherf: Bechtler, $1," 30 grains, fine, rare.

240 "A. Bechtler, $1," 27 grains, fine, rare.

FOREIGN GOLD COINS.

241 1670 German Quadruple Ducat, Leopold, face value $8.80, very fine. rare.

242 1773 Spanish Doubloon, face value $15.50, fine.

243 1798 ½ Joe, Portugal, face value $8.50 uncirculated.

244 Japanese Cobang, oval, face value about $5 00, length 2¾ in., very fine, rare.

245 Japanese ¼ Cobang, oval, value $1.25, length 1⅜ in., fine, rare.

246 Japanese Gold Itzebue, value $2.50, fine, rare.

247 "   "   ½   "   "   1.25, "   "

248 "   Gold Piece, 1 Yen, size of Gold Dollar, new issue, uncirculated.

249 Japanese Gold Dollar, over 300 years old, fair, rare.
250 Medal. Obverse, Bust of Dom Pedro II, of Brazil, reverse, laurel wreath, surrounded by the legend, "*Academia Das Bellas Artes Do Rio De Janeiro.*" Centre in four lines, "*Ao Venia E. A. Applicacao.*" value in gold $10.00, proof, size 16, very rare.
251 1787 Spade Guinea, George III, pierced at top, gold value $5.00 (cost owner $10,) fine, very rare.
252 1786 Half Guinea, George III, good, scarce.
253 1656 ½ Doubloon, Ferdinand III, gold value $2.00, large and thin, uncirculated, rare.
254 1867 Papal coin, 20 Lire, gold value $4.00, fine, rare.
255 1616 German religious medalet, obverse, Crossed swords crowned. Reverse, "I. H. S.", an eye, eagle, &c., large and thin, gold value $2.00, uncirculated.
256 1777 Papal Coin, ½ Doppia of Italy, gold value $1.50, fine, rare.
256½ Republic of Nuremberg, Ducat, gold value $2.20, uncirculated, very rare.
257 1639 Ducat of Saxony, gold value $2.20, fine, rare.
258 1786 1 Convent Kreuz, Germany, value in gold about $1.00, fine, rare.
259 1785 Charles III, ⅛ of a Doubloon, pierced, otherwise good.
260 1775 Charles III, 1/16 of a Doubloon, uncirculated, scarce
261 1786   "   "   "   "   pierced, otherwise good.
262 1786   "   "   "   "   fair.
263 1860 Republic of Mexico, Pistole, gold value $3.75, very fine, proof surface, rare.
264 1869 Republic of Mexico, ½ Pistole, fine, scarce.
265 1833 Republica de Colombia, ½ Pistole, gold value $1.87 very good, scarce.
266 1836 Republica de Colombia, ¼ Pistole, gold value about 90 cents, pierced, fair,
267 East India gold piece, value $1.00, fine.
268   "   "   "   "   "   "   poor.

ENGLISH SILVER COINS.

(The following lots (269 to 370,) present an excellent opportunity to secure a series of the large Silver Coins.)

269 1696 William III, Crown, very good, scarce.
270 16— Same as last, latter part of date not discernable, otherwise good, scarce.
271 1702 Anna, Half Crown, good, rare.

1707 Anna, Crown, good, rare.
1804 Bank of England Dollar, large planchet, very good, scarce.
1804 Bank of England Dollar, smaller planchet, double Strike, very good, scarce.
1804 Bank of England Dollar, still smaller size, fine, scarce.
1804 Bank of England Dollar, smaller than last, fine, scarce.
1820 George III, Crown, St. George and the Dragon, good, scarce.
1821 George IV, Crown, St. George and the Dragon, very good, scarce.
1822 George IV, Crown, same as last.
1811 George III, 3 Shilling Bank Token, good, scarce.
1819 George III, Crown, St. George and the Dragon, fair, scarce.
1826 George IV, Half Crown, fine, pierced.
1834 William IV, Half Crown, fine.
1836   "   "   "   "   good.
1844 Victoria Half Crown, good.
1845   "   "   "   "
1845   "   Crown, uncirculated, scarce.
1845   "   "   "   very good.
1846   "   Half Crown, fine.

FRENCH SILVER COINS.

1726 Louis XV, Crown, good, scarce
1727   "   "   "   fair,   "
1728   "   "   "   good,   "
1762   "   "   "   "   "
1763   "   "   "   good.
1773   "   "   "   very good, scarce.
1791   "   "   "   good, pierced.
1809 Napoleon, 5 Francs, good, rare.
1811   "   "   "   "   pierced, rare.
1812   "   "   "   "   rare.
1813   "   "   "   "   rare.
1815 Louis XVIII, 5 Francs, fine, scarce.
1816   "   "   "   "   "   "
1817   "   "   "   "   good,   "
1820   "   "   "   "   "   "
1821   "   "   "   "   "   pierced, scarce.
1823   "   "   "   "   fine, scarce.
1824   "   "   "   "   good, scarce.

9⅄ 308   1826 Charles X, 5 Francs, good, scarce.
"   309   1828   "   "   "   "   fine,   "
"   310   1830   "   "   "   "   "   "
"   311   1831 Louis Phillippe I, 5 Francs, very fine, scarce.
"   312   1833   "   "   "   "   "   good.   "
"   313   1834   "   "   "   "   "   "   "
"   314   1835   "   "   "   "   "   "   ' "
"   315   1837   "   "   "   ..   "   "   "
    316   1838   "   "   "   "   "   "   "
"   317   1840   "   "   "   "   "   "   "
"   318   1841   "   "   "   "   "   fine,   "
"   319   1844   "   "   "   "   "   "   "
"   320   1845   "   "   "   "   "   good.   "
"   321   1846   "   "   "   "   "   "   "
"   322   1847   "   "   "   "   "   uncirculated.
"   323   1849 Republic, Bust of Liberty, 5 Francs, reverse,
             "*Liberté, Egalité, Fraternité*," fine, scarce.
"   324   1849 Republic, 5 Francs, reverse, 1 male 2 female em-
             blematical figures, fine, scarce.
"   325   1867 Napoleon III, 5 Francs, uncirculated.
"   326   1868   "   "   "   "   "
"   327   1869   "   "   "   "   "
/ 00 328 1870   "   "   "   "   "
"   329   1873 Republic, 5 Francs, reverse, emblematical figures,
             uncirculated, scarce.
"   330   1877 Republic, 5 Francs, reverse, emblematical figures,
             uncirculated, scarce.

SPANISH SILVER COINS.

" 331   1758 Ferdinand VI, "Pillar Dollar", very fine, pierced,
             Rare.
" 332   1761 Charles III, "Pillar Dollar", very fine, scarce.
" 333   1770   "   "   "   "   fine but pierced,
             scarce.
" 334   1778 Charles III, Dollar, good.
   335   1780   "   "   "   "
   336   1781   "   "   "   "
   337   1785   "   "   "   "
   338   1786   "   "   "   "
   339   1787   "   "   "   "
   340   1788   "   "   "   "   pierced.
   341   1789   "   "   "   "
" 342   1790 Charles IV, Dollar, good.
" 343   1791   "   "   "   "   pierced.

8/ 314	1793 Charles IV, Dollar, good.	
" 315	1794 " " " "	
" 316	1795 " " " "	
" 317	1796 " " " "	
" 348	1797 " " " "	
" 349	1798 " " " "	
" 350	1799 " " " "	
" 351	1800 " " " "	
" 352	1801 " " " "	
" 353	1802 " " ' " "	
" 354	1803 " " " "	
" 355	1804 " " " "	
" 356	1805 " " " "	
" 357	1806 " " " "	
" 358	1808 " " " fine.	
" 359	1809 Ferdinand VII, Dollar. fine.	
" 360	1810 " " " "	
" 361	1811 " " " "	
" 362	1816 " " " "	
363	1817 " " " "	
" 364	1819 " " " good.	
" 365	1820 " " " "	
" 366	1821 " " " very fine.	
" 367	1822 " " " good.	
97 368	1850 Isabella, 20 Reals, fine.	
" 369	1856 Ferdinand II, Dollar, fine.	
150 370	1871 Amadeo, 5 Pesetas, fine.	

COPPER COINS OF GREAT BRITAIN.

55 371 1797 Two Pence, George III, very fine, scarce.
80 372 1797 One Penny, " " " " "
10 373 1799 " " " " uncirculated "
" 374 1806, '07, Pennies, " " good and fine, 2 pieces
2 375 1825, '6, '31, '4. '41, '4, '5, '7, '53, '4, '8, Pennies,
 George IV, and Victoria, good to fine, 11 pieces.
5 376 1603 Half Penny, William III, fair, scarce.
2 377 1717, '18, '19, '20, '1, '2, '3, '4, '8, '9, '30, '1, '4, '5, '7,
 '8, '40, '3, '4, '5, '6, '7, '9, '50, '2, '3, '6, '7, '70, '1, '2,
 '3, '4, '5, '8, '81, '7, '9, all Half Pennies, George I
 to George III, good to fine, 37 pieces.
" 378 1825, '6, '7, '31, '4, '8, '41, '4, '6, '7, '52, '3, '4, '7, Half
 Pennies, George IV to Victoria, good to fine,
 14 pieces.

379   1860, '1, '2. '3. '5, '6, '7, '8, '70, '2. '3, '4, '5, Pennies,
Victoria, fine to uncirculated, 13 pieces.

380   1860, '1. '2, '3, '4, '5, '6, '7. '8, '70, '1, '2, '4, '6, Half
Pennies, Victoria, very fine to uncirculated, 14 pieces

381   William and Mary Farthing, obverse, good, reverse,
poor, rare.

382   1672 Charles I, Farthing, good, rare.

383   1674   "   "   "   fair.

384   1717, '22, '31, '6, '49, '54, '73, '5, '99 rare, 1806 Farthings, George I to George III, good to very. fine,
10 pieces.

385   1821, '2 '3, '6, '7, '8, '9, '30, '1, '3; '5. '6. '8, '9, '40, '1,
'2, '3, '4, '5, '7, '8, '50, '1, '4, '6. '7, '60, '1, '2, '3, '4,
'5, '6, '7, '9. '71, '2, '3. '5. George IV to Victoria,
fine to uncirculated, 40 pieces.

386   1828, '35, '44, Half Farthings, George IV to Victoria.
very fine, 3 pieces.

4 387   1805 to 1825 English Hibernia Pennies. (Harp,) good,
5 pieces.

1 388   1753 to 1822 English Hibernia ½ Pennies, (Harp,) good.
27 pieces.

8 389   1750, 1816 English Hibernia Farthings, (Harp,) fine,
2 pieces.

COPPER COINS OF FRANCE, SPAIN, &C.

3/4 390   1768, 71, 80, 1, 5, 9, 71, (3 varieties.) 92, (3 varieties.)
93, (4 varieties) 99, Louis XV and XVI, good to
fine, largest copper and brass coins, 17 pieces.

391   1825 Ten and Five Centimes Charles X, fine, 2 pieces.

392   1827   "   "   "   "   "   "   2   "

393   1828   "   "   "   "   "   "   2   "

394   1839, 41, 3, 4 ; same (in pairs,) Louis Phillippe, 8 pieces.

395   1829 and 30, Five Centimes,   "   "   fine,
2 pieces.

396   4 large brass and one small, Rep. Française, good,
5 pieces.

397   1852, 3, 4, 5, 6, 7, 61, 2, 3, Napoleon III, Ten Centimes,
fine to uncirculated, 9 pieces.

398   1871, 2, 4, Republic, Ten Centimes, uncirculated, 3 pieces.

399   Small Copper Bourbon Coin, "Double Tournois," good,
very rare.

400   1606 Small Copper Coin, Henry IV, "Double Tournois,"
good, very rare.

&401 1739 Colony of Cyane, Two Sous, Copper Coins, good, scarce, 2 pieces.
"402 1808 Napoleon, 10 Centimes, fine, rare.
"403 1809   "   Centesimo, good,   "
"404 1810   "   10 Centimes, "   "
"405 1811   "   "   "   "   "
&406 1846, 8, 9, 50, 1, Un Centime Republic, uncirculated, 4 pieces.
/407 1853, 4, 5, 6, 7, 61, 2, 3, 4, Napoleon III, 5 Centimes, fine to uncirculated, 9 pieces.
"408 1871, 4, Republic, 5 Centimes, uncirculated, 2 pieces.
"409 1854, 5, 6, 7, 61, 62, Napoleon III, good to uncirculated, 6 pieces.
"410 1854, 5, 7, Same, 1 Centime, fine, rare, 3 pieces.
"411 1872 Republic, 1 Centime, fine, rare.
&412 1604 King Phillip, rude, but interesting coin, good.
&413 1774, 5, 84, 97, 1812, 14, 15, 16, 17, 18, 19, 20, (2 var.) 1, 3, 4, 5, 6, 7, 30, 1, 2, 3, 6, 37 (2 var.) 8, 9, 41, Charles III to Isabella, obverse, bust, reverse, arms, good to very fine, 29 pieces.
/414 1848, 51, 67 "5 Decimas," Isabella, good, 3 pieces.
"415 1868 5 Centimos, Isabella, uncirculated, scarce.
-416 Large Coins, various, poor to fine, 4 pieces.
/417 1579 King Phillip, small thin coin, good, rare.
418 1613, 26, 43, King Phillip, large thin coins, good, rare, 3 pieces.
&419 1790 to 1868 medium size copper Coins, all different, good to uncirculated, 23 pieces.
/420 1720 to 1860 small copper Coins, all different, good to uncirculated.

COPPER COINS OF ITALY.

/5 421 1785 to 1801 Papal Coins, large, good, 3 pieces.
/422 1837, 9, 50, 1, same, (1 Baiocco,) fine to uncirculated, 4 pieces.
/422½ Four large and small coins, various, good.
/423 1825, 31, 9, 40, 9, (10 Tornesi) large thick coins, good to very fine.
424 1832, 59, (5 Tornesi,) good.
/425 1866, 7, Pius IX, Four and Two Soldi, uncirculated, 3 pieces.
426 1861, 2, 3, 4, 7, Victor Emanuel, 10 Centesimi, fine, 5 pieces.

427   1863 Victor Emanuel, 50 Centesimi, German silver,
        good, rare.
428   1861, 7, Victor Emanuel, 1 Centesimo, uncirculated,
        2 pieces.
429   Interesting collection of small Italian coins, Ancient and
        Modern, good to uncirculated, 50 pieces.

COPPER COINS OF BRAZIL, &C.

430   1827, 8, 9, 30, 2, "80 Reis," good to fair, 5 pieces.
431   1778, 96, 99, 1802, 16, (2 varieties, 26, 7, 8, 9, 30, 1, 2,
        "40 Reis," good to fine, 13 pieces.
432   1697, 99, "20 Reis," good, rare, 2 pieces.
433   1775, 81, 95, "20 Reis," fine, scarce, 3 pieces.
434   1738, 1819, "10 Reis," good, 2 pieces.
435   1812, 20, 21, "Public Utility" "40 Reis" very thick Coins,
        brass, good, 3 pieces.
436   1823, 4, 5, "Public Utility" "40 Reis," very thick Coins,
        brass, good, 3 pieces.
437   Lot large thick Coins, copper and brass, all different,
        good to fine, 17 pieces.
438   Lot Large thin Coins, good to fine, all different, 17 pieces.
439   Lot Small thin Coins, good to fine, 17 pieces.

AMERICAN AND FOREIGN MEDALS

440   Obverse, bust of Grant, reverse, "Patient of Toil, &c."
        bronze proof, this is the rare Swiss medal by Bovy,
        Size 38.
441   West front of Ely Cathedral, reverse, west view of the
        Choir, bronze proof, size 38.
442   Bust Louis Phillippe, reverse, 3 female figures, Liberty,
        Equality, &c., bronze, fine, size 36.
443   Bust of Joseph Hayden, reverse, Lyre, &c., fine iron
        cast, size 31.
444   Obverse, Mary, Joseph and Child, &c., reverse, a Chalice
        surrounded by sacred Hearts, Angels, cross bones.
        skull, &c , copper, good, size 30.
445   Over lapped busts, Victoria and Albert, 1855; reverse,
        busts of Napoleon and Eugenie, bronze, fine, size 34
446   Bust of Gen. Lafayette, reverse, "The Defender of
        American and French Liberty, 1777—1824", silver,
        fine, size 29.

£0 447 Bust of William Pitt, reverse, "the man who having saved, &c.," copper, thin, scarce, size 26.

/5 148 Fredericus, Prussia, reverse, figures of Fame, Prudence, Virtue, &c., brass, fair, size 30.

6 449 Ditto, Equestrian figure, reverse, battles, &c., brass, pierced, good, size 30.

/0 450 English copper medal, bust of Edward I, reverse, Temple of Fame, fair condition, original, very rare, size 24.

" 451 English copper medal, bust of Henry VII, reverse, monument, born, died, &c., good, rare, size 24.

452 Bust of Edward III, otherwise same as last, cost $20.

453 Bust of William, King of Prussia, reverse, monument, battles, flags, &c., copper, proof, size 25.

454 English Silver War Medal, with silver buckle, inscribed "North West Frontier." Bust of Victoria, reverse, Fame crowning a soldier, presented to R. H. Dillon, Drummer, H. M's. 19th Regt., silver value about $1.50, length 2½ inches.

/ 5V 455 English War Medal, (one buckle,) Sebastopol, silver value about $1.50, very good, length 2½ inches.

UNITED STATES COPPER CENTS

7V5 456 1793 Vine and bars, open leaf twig, inclines slightly to the right, small date, small close "Liberty", hair profuse and flowing nearly straight back, fine condition, good color, slightly worn on hair, reverse, very fine, rare.

£5V 457 1793 Same variety with exception of twig, the leaves of which are narrower and more erect, very good, rare.

/75 458 1793 Vine and bars, large letters, broad date, broad leaved erect twig, weak date, otherwise good, rare.

459 1793 Lettered edge, small Liberty, small twig inclining to the right, small broad date, very good, rare.

460 1793 Vine and Bars, small Liberty, twig has a base horizontal line, small broad date, good.

5 5V 461 1793 "Ameri" variety, good on both sides, good color, very rare.

£00 462 1793 Chain variety, very fair, date plain, rare.

CC5 463 1793 Liberty Cap, perfect die, good, very rare.

464 1794 The celebrated "Starred" variety. This piece is considered the second best of this variety yet discovered. Good both sides. 87 stars on obverse between milling. Excessively rare, only 4 specimens known.

25 465   1794 Head of 1793. Maris. No. 1. Poor.
90 466   1794 Young Head. No. 5. Very good.
100 467   1794 Crooked 7. No. 9. Very fair.
.. 468   1794 Many Haired. No. 11. Good.
75 469   1794 Separated Date. No. 15. Good.
160 470   1794 Ornate. No. 17. Fine, dark.
1,05 471 1794 Venus No. 19. Plain hair-string, uncirculated, light olive.
20 472   1794 Fallen 4. No. 20. Good,
100 473   1794 Short Bust. No. 22. Good, black.
5 474   1794 Large Planch. No. 28. Has plain hair-string, good.
80 475   1794 Shielded Hair. No. 32. Very good.
.. 476   1794 Roman Plica. No. 38. Good.
9 477   1794 Head of 1795. No. 39. Much circulated, but distinct.
.. 478   1794 Treplined Head. No. 42. Very good, rare.
Par 175 479 1794 Young Head. No. 54. Fine, rare.
100 480   1795 Thick planchet, lettered edge, very good, scarce.
" 481   1795   "   "   "   "   wide date, very good scarce.
110 482   1795 Medium planchet, "one cent" high in wreath, dark, fine.
55 483   1795 Medium planchet, "one cent" centre of wreath, small date, good.
Sur 100 484 1795 Thin planchet, "one cent" high in wreath, fine.
.. 485   1795   "   "   "   "   "   broad date good.
Par 125 486 1795 Thin planchet, "one cent" centre of wreath, large letters, fine.
70 487   1795 Thin planchet, "one cent" high in wreath, small letters, very good.
..125 488 1795 Thin planchet, "one cent" centre of wreath, large date, small letters, fine.
489   1795 Thin planchet, "one cent" centre of wreath, small date, small letters, fine.
20 490   1795 Thin planchet, "one cent" centre of wreath, 5 attatched to bust, very good.
..7 491   1795 Thin planchet, "one cent" centre of wreath, 5 distant from bust, good.
70 492   1796 Liberty Cap, very good.
" 493   1796   "   "   "   "   variety in tie of wreath.
40 494   1796   "   "   large close date, good.
25 495   1796   "   "   broad date, good.
.. 496   1796   "   "   double dated, has date very distinct, above and below Liberty, reverse reads, "Of Americt- ates of Ameriates" a rare curiosity, well struck, pierced.

1796 Fillet Head, reverse, "one cent" high in wreath, fine.

1796 Fillet Head, reverse, "one cent" lower in wreath, fine, rare.

1796 Fillet Head, broken die, very good, "one cent" in centre of wreath.

(Continued in Second day's Sale.)

UNITED STATES SILVER DOLLARS.

1794. A good dollar for this excessively rare date. Obverse, Head of Liberty, stars, legend and date all plain. Like nearly all dollars of this date, weak impression on the left of obverse and reverse.

1795. Fillet Head; broad space between stars and date, Very fine. Scarce.

1795. Fillet Head; narrow space between stars and date. Not quite as fine as last Scarce.

1795. Flowing Hair; reverse has small open leaf wreath, unconnected at top, uncirculated, slightly marked with cabinet friction, rare.

1795. Flowing Hair; reverse has large narrow leaved wreath, quite different from last in topmost twigs of wreath, and one berry to the right of Eagle's feet, fine. Scarce.

1795. Flowing Hair; another variety on obverse and reverse, with two berries to right of Eagle's feet, fine.

1795. Flowing Hair; a slight difference in wreath from preceding, fine.

1796. Small date, large letters on reverse, unusually good, nearly fine, scarce.

1797. 6 stars facing, even sharp impression, uncirculated. Small stars, rare.

1797. 7 stars facing, good.

1798. Small Eagle, 13 stars, unusually good, even impression both sides, rare.

1798. Small Eagle, 15 stars, slight puncture, size of pin head, partly through lower field of reverse. Obverse very good, reverse considerably worn, very rare.

1798. Wide date, uncirculated, scarce.

1798 Close date, dotted 9, fine.

1798. " pointed 9, good.

1798. " " " cracked die, good.

516 1799. 5 stars facing, very fine and rare.
517 1799. 6 "   "   cracked die, wide date, good.
518 1799. "   "   "   close date, fine, small nick obv.
519 1799. "   "   "   blunt 9's on obverse, fine.
520 1799. "   "   "   pointed 9's on obverse, fine.
521 1800. Fine, sharp, date regular.
522 1800. Fine, sharp, date irregular, cipher above the line of 18. Scarce.
523 1801. Fine, scarce.
524 1802. Perfect date, nearly fine, scarce.
525 1802. Over 1, good, slightly tarnished.
526 1802. " 1, slight crack in die, good.
527 1803. Bright and uncirculated, slight cabinet friction, scarce.
528 1803. Variety in position of stars, good.
529 18)4. Silver plated copy.
530 1836. Dull proof, slightly worn, rare.
531 1838. Sharp brilliant proof, excessively rare. (Pattern.)
532 1839.   "   "   "   "   "   "
533 1840. Fine.
534 1841. "
535 1812. Very fine.
536 1843 Uncirculated.
537 1844 Very fine.
538 1845 Fine.
539 1846 Very fine.
540 1847 Fine.
541 1848 Very fine.
542 1849   "   "
543 1850 Uncirculated.
544 1851 Very fine, very rare
545 1852 Fine, very rare. (The last two lots are in about equal condition, and both sharp and beautiful pieces, and rarely found in a Coin Sale.)
546 1853 Fine, scarce.
547 1854 Very fine and rare.
548 1855 Dull proof, rare.
549 1856 Very fine, rare.
550 1857 Brilliant proof, very rare.
      (1858 Dollar will be found under the head of Proof Sets.)
551 1859 Very fine.
552 1860 Dull proof.
553 1861 Uncirculated.
554 1862 Good.
555 1863 Brilliant proof.

1861 Fine, but dark.
1865 Pierced, fair.
1866 Uncirculated.
1867 Good.
1868 Good.
1869 Fine.
1870 Very good.
1871 Uncirculated.
1872   "
1873 Liberty seated, fine.
1873 Trade, brilliant proof.
1874 Trade, very fine, very peculiar obverse, has a
        nude figure of Liberty, not the work of U. S. Mint,
        but a genuine dollar.
1875 Brilliant proof.
1876 Fine.
1877 Uncirculated.
1878 Trade, uncirculated.
1878 Bland, uncirculated.
1879   "   "
1879 Trade, proof, rare.

AMERICAN AND FOREIGN WHITE METAL MEDALS.

1866 Bust of Martin Luther, reverse, "1st American
        Conference at St. Georges Church, Phila " proof,
        size 32.
1869 "50th Ann'y I. O. O. F., Phila., April 26,"
        pierced, fine, size 32.
Bust of Humbolt, by Pacquet, reverse, "Earth and
        Heaven He Explored," &c., proof, size 32.
Bust of Bishop Soule, by Key, reverse, "Push Forward
        The Great Work," proof, size 32.
Victoria Bridge, Montreal, reverse, Medallion portraits of
        Victoria, Prince of Wales, Prince Albert, &c., proof,
        size 32.
1876 Centennial Exhibition, (Phila.) obverse, Declara-
        tion of Independence, reverse, views of Memorial Hall,
        Main Building and Horticultural Hall, proof, size 32
1876 View of Independence Hall, reverse, Memorial
        Hall. In glass case, showing both sides, proof, size 36.
1876 View of Main Building, (Phila. Centennial,) re-
        verse, Art Gallery and Fairmount Park. In glass
        case, showing both sides, proof, size 32.

2⁵583   1869 Bust of Grant, reverse, "Inauguarated March 4th,"
&c., proof, size 32.
⁵584   1869 Same, with ribbon, pierced.
8⁰585   1865 Bust of Lincoln, reverse, "He is in Glory and the
Nation in tears," proof, scarce, size 32.
6⁻586   1861, 2 Bust of McClellan, reverse, description of
battles, proof, size 30.
" 587   Bust of Henry Clay, reverse, Fame inscribing a monument. Legend : "Every end he aimed at was his
Country's," proof, rare, size 26.
" 588   1865 Firemen's Parade, Phila., reverse, Fire Engine,
proof, pierced, size 32.
2⁵589   Shield shape medal, suspended from a buckle, obverse,
Masonic emblems, reverse, Masonic Temple, N. Y.
"Dedicated June 2nd, 1875," proof, length 2½ inches
scarce.
/⁰590   1875. Bunker Hill Medalet, suspended from an eagle,
proof, size 16.
" 591   Bust of Grant, surrounded by stars, wreath, &c., reverse
eagle, flags, presented to Benj. Lane Co. M., 6 Pa.
Heavy Artillery, proof, pierced, size 18.
2⁰592   Same to Sam'l Strawhecher, Co. B, 133 Regt., Ind. Vols.
9 A. C.
/2 593   Same to Enzly Babb, unattached Me. Vols., 9 A. C.
" 594   "   " Abr. Hebber, Co. I, 133 Regt. Ind. Vols. 9 A. C.
" 595   "   " Jno. M. Wilds, 4 Mass. Heavy Art'y.
" 596   "   " Geo. W. Cooly, 30 Co., unattached Heavy Art'y,
Mass. Vols.
" 597   Same to Dennis Leary, unattached Me. V. V. 19th A. C.
" 598   "   " Syl. Mathias, Co. I, 201 Regt Pa. Vols, 22 A. C.
/⁰599   Centennial, Eagle, Shield, &c. rev. " Dedicated to the
people of the U. S.," proof, size 24.
⁵600   View Dec. of Ind., reverse, Commemoration of Centennial,
· proof, size 24.
6 601   1876, Goddess of Lib., reverse, birth-place of Independence, proof, size 22.
" 602   1876, Same, reverse, American Colonies, proof, size 22.
" 603   1875, Centennial Main Building, reverse, illustrating 100
years' growth, proof, size
" 604   Milt. Bust. Ant. Wayne, reverse, Brandywine, &c. proof,
size 22.
" 605   Bust of Fulton, reverse first steamboat Hudson River,
1807, proof, size 22.
" 606   1857. Bust of Luther, reverse, " 7th Jubilee," proof, size
24.

COIN SALE CATALOGUES, &C., UNPRICED.

(All clean and perfect—All numismatic, unless otherwise named.)

607	1859 May 4, 5.	W. L. Bramhall, New York.
608	1863 Jan. 26.	McGuire & Co., Washington.
" 609	1870 May 19.	M. W. Dickeson. Philadelphia.
" 610	1870 September 8.	Mason & Co., New York.
611	1871 April 21.	Leavitt & Co, New York.
" 612	1871 November 7.	Mason & Co., Philadelphia.
613	1872 April 8, 9, 10.	" " "
" 614	1872 April 11, 12.	Benj. Haines, New York.
" 615	1872 May 7, 8.	E. J. Cleveland, " "
" 616	1873 April 9.	Alex. Balmano, Philadelphia.
" 617	1873 June 9, 10, 11.	Ed. Cogan, New York.
" 618	1873 September 22, 23.	Bangs & Co. New York.
" 619	1873 October 13, 14.	F. H. Shultze, " "
" 620	1873 November 20, 21.	Ed Cogan, New York.
" 621	1874 February 17, 18, 19.	(Campbell) Haseltine. Phila.
622	1874 May 5, 6, 7, 8.	(Jas. Parker,) Cogan, New York.
623	1874 June 17.	Hagadorn, New York.
" 624	1874 September 24.	Ed. Cogan, New York.
625	1874 December 16, 17.	Ed. Cogan, New York.
" 626	1874 December 21, 22, 23.	C. D. Lathrop, New York.
627	1875 January 25, 6, 7, 8.	J. W. Haseltine, " "
628	1875 March 1, 2,	J. W. Haseltine, New York.
629	1875 April 13, 14.	" " Philadelphia.
630	1875 April 28, 29, 30, May 1.	J. E. Gray (Strobridge), New York.
" 631	1875 May 7.	Ed. Cogan, New York.
632	1875 June 30.	" " " "
633	1875 July 12.	J. W. Haseltine, Philadelphia.
" 634	1875 October 7.	" " "
635	1875 October, 25, 6, 7, 8.	Col. Cohen (Cogan,) New York.
636	1875 December 6, 7, 8, 9.	J. W. Haseltine, Phila.
637	1876 March 30.	(Part 1st Centl.) J. W. Haseltine, Philadelphia.
638	1876 April 17. 18.	Ed. Cogan, New York.
639	1876 April 24.	(Part 2d Centl.) J. W. Haseltine, Philadelphia.
640	1876 May 2, 3, 4.	Geo. H. Farrier, New York.
641	1876 May 16,	(Part 3d Centl.) J. W. Haseltine, Philadelphia.
642	1876 June 29, 30.	Ed. Cogan, New York.

6 643   1876 July 17, 18, (Part 4th Centl.) J. W. Haseltine, Philadelphia.

4 644   1876 September 6, 7, 8. (Part 5th Centl.) J. W. Haseltine, Philadelphia.

3 645   1876 September 14, 15. D. Proskey, New York.

6 646   1876 September 19, 20, 21. (Part 6th Centl.) J. W. Haseltine, Philadelphia.

4 647   1876 October 30, 31, Nov. 1. Henry S. Adams (Cogan) New York.

5 648   1876 November 6, 7, 8. (Part 7th Centl.) J. W. Haseltine, Philadelphia.

3 649   1876 December 18, 19. Ed. Cogan, New York.

" 650   1877 February 1, 2.   "   "   "   "

5 651   1877 February 12, 13, 14, 15. J. W. Haseltine, Philadelphia.

4 652   1877 March 8, 9. Stenz Collection (Strobridge,) New York.

3 653   1877 April 12 13. Ed. Cogan, New York.

5 654   1877 May 17, 18.   "   "   "   "

3 655   1877 May 28, 29. Ferguson Haines, New York.

5 656   1877 June 11, 12, 13. J. W. Haseltine, Philadelphia.

3 657   1877 June 28, 29. Ed. Cogan, New York.

" 658   1877 September 5, 6. (Paper Money,) J. W. Haseltine, Philadelphia.

" 659   1877 September 17, 18. Ed. Cogan, New York.

6 660   1877 October 22, 23, 24, 25. J. B. Clemens (Cogan,) New York.

3 661   1877 October 23, 24. Scott & Co. New York.

6 662   1877 October 25, 26. Dr. Grotefend, (Harzfeld.) New York.

6 663   1877 November 7, 8, 9. Ed. Cogan, New York.

6 664   1877 November 30, Dec. 1. Ed. Cogan, New York.

6 665   1877 December 5, 6, 7. Scott & Co., New York.

6 666   1877 December 20, 21. Ed. Cogan, New York.

667   1878 January 7, 8, 9. J. W. Haseltine, Philadelphia.

6 668   1878 January 8, 9. C. W. Idell, (Attinelli,) New York.

5 669   1878 January 23, 24. Ed. Cogan, New York.

3 670   1878 February 25, 26, 27. J. W. Haseltine, Philadelphia.

" 671   1878 February 27, 28. Ed. Cogan, New York.

" 672   1878 March 4, 5, 6. A. Redlich (Scott & Co.) New York.

" 673   1878 March 19, 20, 21. Snow Collection (Strobridge,) New York.

674 1878 April 24, 25. Paper Money and Autos. (Haseltine) Philadelphia.

675 1878 May 6, 7, 8, 9. J. Swan Randall (Cogan,) New York.

676 1878 June 17, 18, 19. T. R. Strobridge, New York.

677 1878 June 27, 28. Ed. Cogan, New York.

678 1878 June 30, 31. Scott & Co., " "

679 1878 September 16, 17, 18, 19, 20. Ed. Cogan, New York.

680 1878 October 10. Scott & Co., New York.

681 1878 October 22, 23, 24, 25. J. B. Clemens (Cogan,) New York.

682 1878 October 30, 31. J. W. Haseltine, Philadelphia.

683 1878 November 5, 6. J. J. Mickley (E. Mason, Jr.) Philadelphia.

684 1878 November 16. (Paper Money,) Bechtel, New York.

685 1878 December 9, 10. Scott & Co., New York.

686 1878 December 16, 17, 18. Roet Cabinet (Cogan,) New York.

687 1879 January 15, 16, 17. J. W. Haseltine, New York.

688 1879 January 31. J. W. Haseltine, New York.

689 1879 February 28. Ed. Cogan, New York.

690 1879 March 3, 4, 5, 6, 7, 8. S. B. Schieffelin (Scott & Co.,) New York.

691 1879 April 17, 18. L. White (Cogan,) New York.

692 1879 May 1, 2. M. Moore (Cogan,) " "

693 1879 May 21, 22, 23, 24. L. Wilder (Haseltine,) New York.

694 1879 May 29. Ed. Cogan, New York.

695 1879 June 5, 6. S. K. Harzfeld, New York.

696 1879 June 13, 14. Edward Frossard, New York.

697 1879 June 20. Ed. Cogan, New York.

698 1879 July 29, 30. J. W. Haseltine, New York.

699 1879 September 2, 3. Ed. Cogan, New York.

700 1879 September 4. Alf. Watkins (Scott & Co.) New York.

701 1879 September 11, 12. S. K. Harzfeld, New York.

702 1879 September 26. Edward Frossard, " "

703 1879 September 29, 30, Oct. 1. Pratt Collection (Woodward,) New York.

704 1879 October 9. Chapman Bros., New York.

705 1879 October 22, 23. J. W. Haseltine, New York.

706 1879 October 27, 28. Noel Gray (Scott & Co.,) New York.

707 1879 November 7. Edward Frossard, New York.
708 1879 November 17, 18. (Anthony, Part 1st,) Cogan, New York.
709 1879 November 28, 29. J. W. Haseltine, New York.
710 1879 December 1, 2, 3. T. W. Riley (Cogan,) New York.
711 1879 December 15. Scott & Co., New York.
712 1879 December 16, 17, 18, 19. Packer, Gerdts, Mason and Truesdale (Woodward,) New York.
713 1880 January 21. (Second day's Sale,) J. W. Haseltine, New York.
714 1880 January 17. Smith & Sampson, New York.
715 1880 January 28. (Small Pamphlet,) Dowling, Washington.
716 1880 February 10. M. W. Davis, (Scott & Co.,) New York.
717 1880 February 10. (Paper Money,) J. W. Haseltine, New York.
718 1880 February 17. S. K. Harzfeld, Philadelphia,
719 1880 February 27, 28. Stenz Collection (Frossard,) New York.
720 1880 March 22, 23, 24, 25. Carter Cabinet (Bangs & Co.,) New York.
721 1880 April 3 Edward Frossard, New York.
722 1880 April 12. Grunewald, (Scott & Co.,) New York.
723 1880 May 10. Monroe Collection (Haseltine,) Philadelphia.
724 1880 May 17, 18. J. W. Haseltine, Philadelphia.
725 1880 May 28. Ferguson Haines (Chapmans,) New York.
726 1880 June 5. Edward Frossard, New York.
727 1880 June 24, 25. J. W. Haseltine, New York.
728 1880 June 30. Titcomb Collection (Harzfeld,) New York.

SECOND DAY'S SALE.

COLONIAL PAPER MONEY.

CONNECTICUT.

729) 1780 July 1. 1s. 3d., good, rare.

NEW JERSEY.

730) 1776 March 25. 6s. Red ink, watermarked, fine, scarce.

PENNSYLVANIA.

/ 731   1772 April 3.   2s. 6d., good, scarce.
" 732   1772   "   "   2s., good, scarce.
" 733   1772   "   "   1s.,   "   "
" 734   1772   "   "   18d.,   "   "
" 735   Same, different signatures, good, scarce.
" 736   1775 October 25. 9d. good, scarce.
" 737   1775 December 8. 40s., fine.
" 738   1775   "   "   20s.,   "
" 739   1776 April 25.   30s.,   "
" 740   1776   "   "   1s., good.
" 741   1776   "   "   3d., and 9d., good, (different signa-
            tures,) 4 pieces
/ 742   1777 April 10. 4s., Red note, water marked, good,
            scarce.
2 743   1777 April 10. 8s., Red note, water marked, good,
            fine.
/ 744   1777 April 10. 3s. Red note, water marked, good, scarce
5 745   1777   "   "   18d. "   "   "   "   "   "
/ 746   1777   "   "   16s. Black "   "   "   fine   "
4 747   1777   "   "   6s.   "   "   "   "   "   "
" 748   1777   "   "   2s.   "   "   "   "   "   "
6 749   1777   "   "   1s.   "   "   "   "   (unsigned,)
            fine, scarce.
" 750   1777 April 10. 18d. Black note, water marked, scarce.
/ 751   1777   "   "   9d.   "   "   "   "   good   "
8 752   1777   "   "   6d.   "   "   "   "   fine   "
/ 753   1777   "   "   4d.   "   "   "   "   "   "
" 754   1775, 6, 7 April 10, 25. 6d. and 4d., all different, good,
            4 pieces.

DELAWARE.

10 755   1776 January 1. 5s., fine.
11 756   1776   "   "   2s. 6d., fine.
15 757   1777 May 1. 4s., fine.

MARYLAND.

4 758   1756 August 4. "Half a Dollar," different signatures,
            good, scarce, 2 pieces.
/ 759   1770 March 1. $1.00, torn.
  760   1774 April 10. $⅑, fair.
" 761   1775 December 7. $2.00, good.
  762   1775   "   " $1⅓, different signatures, good,
            2 pieces.
/ 763   1776 August 14. $2 00, fine.

VIRGINIA.

761   1773 March 1. Large note, £3, fine, very rare.
765   1776 May 6. 1s. 3d., fine, rare.
766   1776 October 7. $15.00, good, rare.
767   1776 October 7. $10.00,   "   "
768   1776 October 7. $½., fine, rare.
769   1778 May 1. $10.00,   "   "
770   1778 October 5. $7.00, clean, but torn, rare.
771   1779 May 3, Large note, $50.00, clean, very fine,
       excessively rare.
772   1780 July 1. Thin paper, $20.00, clean, very fine, rare.
773   1780 "   "   "   " $15.00,   "   "   "   "
774   1780 "   "   "   " $10.00,   "   "   "   "

SOUTH CAROLINA.

775   1776 December 23, Large note, $8.00, clean, very fine,
       very rare.

CONTINENTAL PAPER MONEY.

776   1775 February 17, $3.00, good,
777   1775 May 10. $3.00, fine.
778   1775 November 29. $7.00, good.
779   1776 May 1. $3.00, good.
780   1776 July 22. $8.00 fine.
781   1778 September 26. $50.00, good.
782   1778 September 26. $7.00,   "
783   1779 January 11. $70.00,   "
784   1779 January 11. $10.00, fine.
785   1776 February 17. $½., varieties, good, 2 pieces.

CONFEDERATE STATES PIECES.

786   1860 Brass Medalet, obverse, Palm Tree, Cotton bales,
       &c., "No submission to the North," reverse, cotton,
       sugar cane, &c., "The wealth of the South," &c., fine.
       size 11.
787   1861 Copper cent (nickel size) obverse Head of Liberty,
       Legend "Confederate States of America, 1861"; Rev.
       "1 Cent" in Laurel wreath, very fine, very rare, cost
       owner $10. Printed explanation, and Ms. of the num-
       ber struck accompanies the piece. Dies by Lovett.
788   1861 Silver Half Dollar (O Mint) Obverse same as ordi-
       nary 1861 Half Dollars, Rev. shield surmounted by
       Liberty Cap surrounded by wreath of sugar cane & cot-
       ton in bloom, Legend, "Confederate States of America

Half Dollar." An excellent specimen from original die, struck by Scott & Co. These silver copies are very rare. Printed certificate accompanies piece.

789 1862 Large gold plated shell, obverse equestrian figure of Washington, within a wreath composed of the staple productions of the South, surrounded by the Legend "The Confederate States of America, 22 Feb. 1862 *Deo Vindice.*" In silver mounted glass cover, enclosed in a velvet lined brass hinged paper maché case, the latter elabatorly ornamented with State and National emblems, proof, size 56.

789½ 1861, Silver medalet, obverse, bust of Davis, letters C. R. beneath the bust, around the border "Jefferson Davis," reverse, "C. S. A., First President," around a laurel wreath, in the centre of which is the date, "1861" very good, excessively rare. fetched $22.50 in a recent N. Y. sale, size 12.

U. S. PATTERN PIECES. &C.

790 1850 Silver Three cent piece, obverse Liberty Cap, reverse III, U. S. of A. fine, rare.

791 1851 Quarter Eagle, silver, very good.

792 1854 Copper cent without stars, proof, scarce.

793 1855 " " flying Eagle, very fine. "

794 1859 Silver Half Dollar obverse, bust of liberty reverse, "Half Dollar", proof, scarce.

795 1866 Nickel Five cent piece, obverse, bust of Washington, reverse, small "5 cents." in a curved line, motto, "In God we trust," very fine, rare.

796 1868 Three cent nickel piece, large planchet, obverse, bust of Liberty, reverse, III, fine scarce.

797 1868 One cent nickle piece, obverse same as last, reverse I, fine, scarce.

798 1873 Six silver proof Dollars, being a set of the Trade Dollar Patterns, only 60 sets struck at U. S. Mint, all different, extremely rare.

799 1836 Feb 22, 1st steam cowage, copper, very fine size 18.

800 1836 March 23, same, very good.

CONTINUATION OF U. S. CENTS.

801 1796 Fillet Head, cracked die, good.

802 1796 "LIIIERTY" variety, good, rare.

803 1796 " " small wreath. fair, rare.

804 1796 " " large wreath. very fair, rare, coarse lines to wreath and tie.

75-805	1797	Beautiful light olive, uncirculated, very rare.
806	1797	Uncirculated, dark, rough planchet, fine lines to wreath and tie, rare.
807	1797	Date touches hair, dark, fine.
808	1797	Close date, fine.
809	1797	Broad date, large planchet, very good.
810	1797	Close date, small planchet, dark, fine.
811	1798	Over '97, fine.
812	1798	Close date, very fine.
813	1798	Large letters in Liberty, very fine.
814	1798	Small " " " fine.
815	1798	Small broad date, fine.
816	1798	Large close date, fine.
817	1798	Small 8, fine.
818	1798	Large 8, "
819	1798	Reverse, Milled edge, very good.
820	1798	Obverse and reverse, milled edge, very good.
821	1799,	98 Variety, fine, very rare.
822	1799	Perfect date, good.
823	1800	Over 1799, fine,
824	1800	Perfect date, fine.
825	1800	Large planchet, fine.
826	1800	Small planchet, "
827	1800	Cracked die, fine.
828	1801	₁⁰⁰ variety, fine.
829	1801	₀⁰⁰ " "
830	1801	₁⁰⁰ over ₀⁰⁰ fine.
831	1801	₁⁰⁰ ciphers distant from the 1, good.
832	1802	₁⁰⁰ uncirculated, sharp, steel color, rare.
833	1802	₁⁰⁰ variety, good, scarce.
834	1802	₁⁰⁰ " fine.
835	1803	Large ₁⁰⁰ uncirculated, bright red, very rare in this condition.
836	1803	Small ₁⁰⁰ fine.
837	1803	Medium ₁⁰⁰ fine.
838	1803	Broken die, good.
839	1804	An excellent impression, obverse and reverse, Broken Die, very good in all respects, rare.
840	1804	Broken Die, good, very plain date, rare.
841	1805	5 touches bust, fine, scarce.
842	1805	5 distant from bust, fine, scarce.
843	1806	Very fine, light olive, slight crack in planchet left of bust, very rare in this condition.
844	1806	An extra sharp impression, very fine, rare.
845	1806	Very fine, light olive color, rare.

1807 over 6, fine, dark color.
1807 Perfect date, fine dark color.
1808 Very fine, very dark.
1808 12 stars fine good color.
1809 Uncirculated, but very dark in color, smooth even surface, very rare in this condition.
1809 Fine good color.
1810 Over nine fine, black.
1810 Very fine, a little corroded.
1810 Large date, fine, good color.
1810 Small broad date, fine, dark color.
1820 Head of Liberty & date both sides. If two parts solder together, very skillfully executed, a curiosity.
1811 Over 10, fine, dark, scarce.
1811 Perfect date, fine, dark, scarce. *Por*
1812 Large date, very fine, good color.
1812 Small date, good color.
1813 Uncirculated, but very black, scarce.
1813 Very fine.
1814 Plain 4, very fine.
1814 Crossed 4, very fine.
1811 Plain 4, fine.
1814 Crossed 4, fine.
1815 Altered from 13 very skillfully executed, good condition.
1815 Altered from 45, very good
1816 Perfect planchet, uncirculated, light olive.
1816 Broken Die uncirculated, bright red.
1817 date to right of Bust, uncirculated, bright red.
1817 "   under Bust   "   "   "
1817 close date, very fine.
1817 broad date,   "
1817 15 stars very good, scarce.
1818 perfect die uncirculated, light olive.
1818 cracked die, no Mint mark, uncirculated, red.
1819 small date, uncirculated, red, proof surface.
1819 large date   "   light olive.
1820 uncirculated, red.
1821   "   slightly bruised on cheek, light olive, shows portions of original color, very rare in this condition.
1822 uncirculated, light olive.

(*Concluded in next day's sale.*)

COPPER COINS OF BRAZIL.

10 883   1829 40 Reis. "Public Utility" Large thick coin, good.
15 884   1830   "   "   "   "   "   "   "   fine
5 885   1831 40 Reis. "Public Utility" Large thick coin, good.
" 886   1832   "   "   "   "   "   "   "   good
7 887   1833   "   "   "   "   "   "   "   "
5 888   1834   "   "   "   "   "   "   "   "
. 889   1832-3 "   "   "   "   "   "   good 2 ps
15 890   1699 Peter II Large copper coin, fair.
'891   1847 - 8 - 9 - 53 - 65 "20 Reis" fine, 5 ps.
/892   1764 - 5 - 74 - 6 - 7 - 99 "10 Reis" very good 6 ps
893   1796 "10 Reis" varieties good 2 ps.
894   —— Lot "10 Reis" 1830 to 52 all different good to fine
        10 ps.
895   —— Lot "XL Reis" thin coins '   "   "   "   "
        5 ps.
896   —— Lot "XX Reis" "   "   "   "   "   "   "
        8 ps.
897   —— Lot "V Reis"   "   "   "   "   "   "   "
        9 ps.
898   1875 Petrus II Brazil 40, 20, 10 Reis, fine, 3 ps.
'899   ——   "   "   "   20, 10,   "   " 3 ps.

COPPER COINS OF RUSSIA,

90 900   1776 10 & 5 Kopeks. 2 Kangaroos supporting shield,
            crown, &c, fine, rare large & small, 2 ps.
40 901   1780 Same as last.
50 902   1832 10 Kopeks, Obv. double eagle, very good, rare.
" 903   1833   "   "   "   "   "   "   "   "
1 904   1759 Large thick coin 5 kopeks, good.
. '905   1763   "   "   "   "   "   "
. 906   1769   "   "   "   "   "   pierced.
1 907   1775   "   "   "   "   "   good.
5 908   1788 Large, thick coin. 5 kopeks, good.
10 909   1791   "   "   "   "   "   "
16 910   1793   "   "   "   "   "   fine.
12 911   1803   "   "   "   "   "   good.
2 912   1831 "5 Kopeks" smaller than previous lots, good.
" 913   1832   "   "   "   "   "   "   "   "
7 914   1834   "   "   "   "   "   "   "   "
" 915   1859   "   "   "   "   "   "   " fine
7 916   1863   "   "   "   "   "   "   "   "
. 917   1865   "   "   "   "   "   "   "   " very fine

10 918	1868	"5 Kopeks" smaller than previous lots, uncirculated
25 919	1762	"4 Kopeks," thick, fair.
920	1841	3	"	Large, thin, fair.
" 921	1843	3	"	"	" good.
" 922	1854	"	"	Small, thick, fine.
" 923	1855	"	"	"	"	"
" 924	1860	"	"	"	"	"
c 925	1797	2 Kopeks, Large, thin, good.
" 926	1801	"	"	"	" fine.
927	1811	"	"	Small, thick, good.
" 928	1817	"	"	"	"	"
" 929	1826	"	"	"	"	"
930	1843	"	"	"	"	"
931	1844	"	"	"	"	"
" 932	1798	1 Kopek	"	thin	"
" 933	1800	"	"	"	thick	"

COPPER COINS OF MEXICO, &C.

6 934	1858	One Cuartilla Large thick coin, good.
" 935	1859	"	"	"	"	" fair.
" 936	1861	"	"	" thin	" fine.
" 937	1829	42, 61, Uncirculated Cuartilla, large thin coins, good, 3 ps.
4 938 *3*	1831, 2, 3, 4, 5, 6, quarter Real, good to fine, 6 ps.
3 939	1874, 5, 6, Un Centavo, fine, 3 ps.
1 940	1830, ½ Real good, scarce.
6 941	1860, 1, 5, Large quarter Real, Chihuahua good, 3 ps.
3 942	1833, 46, small	"	"	"	" 2 "
" 943	1855, 6,	"	"	"	" fine 2 "
" 944	Lot of same, various, fair to good, 7 ps.

AMERICAN & FOREIGN ODDITIES.

30 945	1848	U. S. Cent, very small date & stars, reverse "one cent" very large letters. Remarkable copper cent, probably a counterfeit.
2 946	Reverse of U. S. copper cent in the 30's obverse, incused, uncirculated, original.
60 947	1826 U. S. cent struck on ⅔ of the Planchet, fine.
948	1807 " " " Chinese characters on obverse and reverse, poor
" 949	1810 U. S. cent struck on ⅔ of Planchet, poor.
950	Planchets, having impression of cent, both sides incused, fair, 6 ps.

951   1830 U. S. cent misstruck, good.
952   Small round pieces, containing head of Liberty, cut from
     U. S. copper cents, fair, 4 ps.
953   1591 Florentius, curious brass coin, good.
954   1834, 7, 8 curious copper and German silver U. S. half
     Dollars, all head left, fair to good, 4 ps.
955   Piper & Co. wine card, copper, curious reverse, good.
956   Collection of old and curious American and Foreign large
     and small copper and brass coins, medalets, religious
     pieces, &c., &c., fair to good, 75 pieces.
957   Collection of brass, German silver, white metal, and lead
     copies of Foreign and American halves and quarters,
     fair to good, 56 ps.
958   1863 Dix Rebellion Token, "Shoot him on the spoot"
     (instead of spot) fine, rare.
959   Pair of Cats eyes, Chinese buttons, pearl, very fine, rare.
960   African Shell money, 5 pieces.
961   Small piece of stone from Solomon's Temple.
962   Shells from coast of Africa, fine, 6 ps.
963   Small shell from the sea of Tiberias, fine.
964   Small piece of wood, from Cathedral at Rome.
965   5 small blocks of stone from Pompeii.
966   Piece of wood from which S. S. Great Eastern was built.
967   East India Quill money, 7 pieces.
968   Agnus Dei, Catholic charms and satchel worn on neck,
     from Rome.
969   Fossil shell, 2 inches long, spiral.
970   Card board 8 by 10 inches, containing 18 large and small
     Chinese coins with explanations. (from A. D. 1196 to
     A. D. 1367) old and curious, good, rare.
971   Set of Rude Moorish coins, cast, good 3 ps.
972   " " "   "   " varieties, good 3 ps.
973   " " "   "   "   "   "   " " "
974   " " "   "   "   "   "   " " "
975   " " "   "   "   "   "   " " "
976   " " "   "   "   "   "   " " "
977   " " "   "   "   "   "   " 2 "

ANCIENT SILVER COINS.

ROMAN DENARII.

(CONSULAR.)

978   Aluria, Mars in a quadriga, fine.
979   Aemilia, Equestrian on a Bridge, fine.

55 980 Aquilia, Soldier raising a Woman, very fine, Serrated, rare.
981 Fabia. Cornucopia and arrows crossed, fine, rare.
5 982 Gellia. Quadriga, fair, rare.
983 Marcia. Horse running, fair.
984 Renia. Biga of Goats, fine.
6 985 Rubria Carpentum, Very fine, but one word not on the coin.
986 Sergia. Horsemen holding a head. Very good.
987 Servilia. Two Horsemen, fine.
30 988 Urbinia. Triga. Good, rare.
25 989 Vettia. Victory crowning a trophy, a quinarius, very good, rare.
37 990 Uncertain. Female seated on Bucklers, Birds around her, Fine.
25 991 Clovia. Aes, bifrons. Good.

IMPERIAL

55 992 Julius Caesar. Elephant trampling a Serpent, good.
80 993 Vespasian. Soldier Standing, Good.
994 Domitian, Prince of the youths. Without the Imperial title. Fine, rare.
30 995 Trajan. Soldier standing, fine.
50 996 ———— Dacian Seated Weeping, fair, interesting.
997 Hadrian. Female in curule chair, fine.
17 998 Sabina. Concord Seated, fine, scarce.
999 Antoninus Pius. Priests and altar, fine.
15 1000 Faustina Jr. Fecundity standing, quite perfect.
25 1001 Caracalla, Moneta standing, fine.
51 1002 Geta, Priest and altar, very good.
80 1003 Julia Domna. Hilarity standing, fine.
1004 Probus. Happiness standing, fine, base.

U. S. SILVER HALF DOLLARS.

600 1005 1794 close date, lower curl of hair touches point of star. Tie of wreath distant from milling, nearly fine, boldly struck, rare.
640 1006 1794 Wide date, lower curl passes through star, good in every part, rare.
75 1007 1794 tie of wreath extends to milling, good, rare.
25 1008 1795 close date, hair curl passes through star, uncirculated
111 1009 1795 wide date, curl free from star, very good.
1010 1795 close date, curl touches star, " "
1011 1796 16 stars; an excellent specimen of this very rare coin; date, stars, &c., very bold. Has been plugged at top,

the letter E nicely engraved over the plug, a very desirable piece in any condition.

4,00 1012   1797 very good on obverse and reverse, all the designs, legend and date very distinct, very rare and seldom met with in so good a condition.

4 75 1013   1801 fine for this rare date; hair well defined, date bold, a little weak at top of obverse.

6 25 1014   1802, evenly struck in every part, fine and very rare in this condition.

1015   1803 very fine.

65 1016   1803 fine, reverse slightly different from last.

3 75 1017   1805, over 4, fine, rare.

1 4d 1018   1805, broad perfect date; a good match to last. Star in eagle's beak.

70 1019   1805 Close date, same reverse, very good.

1 50 1020   1805 "   " star not in eagle's beak, fine.

1 00 1021   1805 Small 5, four berries on laurel twig, fine, scarce.

77 1022   1805 Cracked die, very good.

55 1023   1806 Pointed 6, cracked die, reverse fine.

60 1024   1806 Dotted 6, free from bust, laurel passes through eagle's claw, fine.

55 1025   1806 Pointed 6 touches bust, cracked die, obverse, fine.

" 1026   1806 Pointed 6, Laurel twig does not pass through eagle's claw, fine.

5 1027   1806 over 5 good rare.

57 1028   1806, T. Y. in Liberty struck twice, pointed 6, good.

" 1029   1806, same variety in Liberty, dotted 6, good, scarce.

" 1030   1806 dotted 6, large E. in Liberty ; good.

3 25 1031   1807 head right, uncirculated, bright and sharp, cracked die, wide date, scarce.

2 90 1032   1807 head right close date, perfect die, bright sharp and uncirculated.

1 55 1033   1807 Head left, larger planchet than any of the half dollars, nearly fine, rare.

1 05 1034   1807 Head left, ordinary planchet, C distant from 50, fine.

71 1035   1807 head left C Close to 50, good.

55 1036   1808 over 7 very good.

" 1037   1808 perfect date, fine.

57 1038   1808 over 7 cracked die, good.

60 1039   1808 stars on right of obverse extend to milling, scarce.

1 00 1040   1809 uncirculated cracked die.

1041   1809 perfect die, fine.

57 1042   1809 apparently an over date, good.

" 1043   1810 wide date, fine.

1044   1810 close date, good.
1045   1810 cracked die, good.
1046   1810 small date, fine.
1047   1811 Twig leaves distant from 50, fine.
1048   1811 small date fine.
1049   1811 date separated by a point (18. 11) good, scarce.
1050   1811 large close date, good.
1051   1811 large wide date, fine.
1052   1811 small wide date, fine.
1053   1811 same, fine.
1054   1811 same, cracked die, fine.
1055   1812 uncirculated, large 8.
1056   1812 reverse shows overstrike, good.
1057   1812 small 8, good.
1058   1812 separated 2, good.
1059   1812 stars touch milling, fine.
1060   1813 reverse shows an overstrike, uncirculated.
1061   1813 cracked die, fine.
1062   1813 stars touch milling, uncirculated.
1063   1813 E. Pluribus Unum appears under bust, good, scarce.
1064   1813 letters under 50c., uncirculated.
1065   1814 uncirculated.
1066   1814 over 13 fine.
1067   1814 letters under bust, good.
1068   1814 Eagle's wing connected with motto, good, rare.
1069   1814 Double strike, fine.
1070   1815 Uncirculated, sharp, possessing the original Mint
         lustre, very rare.
1071   1815 Showing a double impression which can be seen on
         nearly all pieces of this date, fine, rare.
1072   1817 Regular date, uncirculated.
1073   1817 Date divided (1-81-7), scarce.
1074   1817 Date divided in the middle, (17-), fine, scarce.
1075   1817 Cracked die, double strike, very fine.
1076   1818 Large planchet, double milling, rare, (date thus,
         1-81-8), uncirculated.
1077   1818 Small close date, uncirculated.
1078   1818 Large broad date, very fine.
1079   1819 over '18 Close date, uncirculated.
1080   1819 Perfect close date, very good.
1081   1819 Wide date, very good.
1082   1819 Small 9, very good.
1083   1820 Large 2, cracked die, uncirculated.
1084   1820 over '19 uncirculated, scarce.
1085   1820 Small 2, cracked die, very fine, scarce.

1086	1821	Blunt 2, good, scarce, (base of 2 differs from others)
1087	1821	Perpendicular 50, uncirculated, scarce.
1088	1821	Slanting 50, very good.
1089	1822	Perfect die, uncirculated.
1090	1822	Cracked die, good.
1091	1823	Perfect die, fine.
1092	1823	over '22, very fine.
1093	1823	over '20, good.
1094	1824	over '23, very good.
1095	1824	over '22, L. S. scratched on field, otherwise very fine.
1096	1824	Perfect date, uncirculated.
1097	1824	Date close to bust, differing from preceding '24s, good.
1098	1825	Very fine.
1099	1826	Wide date, uncirculated.
1100	1826	Close date, very fine.
1101	1827	Long tailed 7, fine.
1102	1827	Ordinary 7, uncirculated.
1103	1827	Cracked die, fine.
1104	1827	Misstruck, a curiosity, fine.
1105	1828	Stars touch milling, very fine.
1106	1828	Large date, very fine.
1107	1828	Small date, uncirculated.
1108	1828	Large 8, fine.
1109	1828	Cracked die, good.
1110	1829	over '27 uncirculated.
1111	1829	Perfect date, fine.
1112	1830	Cracked die, uncirculated.
1113	1830	Large 0, very fine,
1114	1830	Small 0, very fine.
1115	1830	Perfect die, uncirculated,
1116	1831	" " " slight variety.
1117	1832	" " " " "
1118	1832	Cracked die, fine.
1119	1832	Overstrike, uncirculated.
1120	1832	Variety in stars facing, fine, scarce.
1121	1833	small 50 uncirculated.
1122	1833	cracked die "
1123	1833	large 50 uncirculated.
1124	1834	large date, "
1125	1834	small date small letters.
1126	1834	large " large letters.
1127	1834	stars touch milling,
1128	1835	small date and letters, uncirculated.

1836 Lettered edge, uncirculated.
1836   "   "   "   proof surface.
1836 Reeded   "   fine, rare.
1837 Cracked die, uncirculated.
1837 Perfect   "   "
1838   "   "   "
1838 Cracked "   "
1839 Head of Liberty, uncirculated.
1839 Liberty seated, very good.
1840 Fine.
1841 O Mint, fine.
1841 P Mint, very good.
1842 "   "   "   "
1842 O "   "   "
1843 Perfect die, uncirculated.
1843 Cracked "   "
1844 P Mint,   "
1844 O "   fine.
1845 "   "   uncirculated.
1845 P "   fine.
1846 "   "   uncirculated, proof surface.
1846 O "   fine.
1847 "   "   very fine.
1847 P "   fine.
1848 "   "   "
1848 date touches bust, fine.
1848 O Mint, fine.
1849 "   "   "
1849 P "   very fine.
1850 "   "   fine.
1850 O "   uncirculated.
1851 "   "   "   scarce.
1852 "   "   "   rare.
1852 P "   very fine.
1853 "   "   "   good
1853 O "   "   "
1854 Fine.
1855 O Mint, fine.
1856 "   "   very good.
1856 P "   "   "
1857 "   "   uncirculated,
1857 O "   very good.
1858 Uncirculated.
1859 Fine.
1859 O Mint, very good.

5) 1174 1860 O Mint, very good.
" 1175 1860 P " fine.
" 1176 1861 " " uncirculated.
" 1177 1861 O " fine.
" 1178 1862 Uncirculated.
75 1179 1863 Brilliant proof.
57 1180 1864 Very good.
58 1181 1864 S. Mint, fine.
55 1182 1865 Very fine.
57 1183 1866 Fine.
110 1183½ 1866 S. Mint, no motto, scarce.
57 1184 1867 Uncirculated.
" 1185 1868 Fine.
" 1186 1869 Uncirculated.
" 1187 1870 "
" 1188 1871 " proof surface.
60 1189 1871 S. Mint, fine.
57 1190 1872 Fine.
" 1191 1873 Uncirculated, (arrows.)
" 1192 1873 Fine, (no arrows.)
" 1193 1873 C. C. Mint, fine.
" 1194 1874 Uncirculated.
" 1195 1875 S. Mint, uncirculated.
" 1196 1876 Uncirculated.
25 1197 1877 S. Mint, uncirculated, proof surface.
57 1198 1878 Uncirculated, proof surface.
" 1199 1879 " scarce.

COPPER COINS, TOKENS, &C., OF THE DOMINION OF CANADA.

2 1200 1816 Brock Token, uncirculated.
4 1201 1816 Half Penny Token, obverse, ship, "Montreal," at top, good, scarce.
3 1202 1820 Half Penny Token, "Commercial Change," good.
1 1203 1823 " " " plow, good.
2 1204 1825 " " " (Bust,) "British Colonies," good.
1 1205 1830 Half Penny Token, obverse, Canada, good.
5 1206 1832 " " " reverse, Province of Upper Canada, fine, scarce.
1 1207 1833 Half Penny Token, plow, reverse, Sloop, good.
5 1208 1833 " " " "Commercial Change," reverse, Sloop, fine.
— 1209 1841 Half Penny, obverse, Canada, good.

2 1210 1855 "One Cent," reverse, Fisheries, &c., fine.
1 1211 1837 One Penny, Montreal, fine.
" 1212 1842 "   "   "   reverse, a banking house, uncirculated.
3 1213 1852 One Penny, Quebec, fine.
" 1214 1850, '2, '4, '7 One Penny, Bank of Upper Canada, uncirculated, 4 pieces.
1 1215 1837, '52 Half Penny, Quebec, varieties, fine.
" 1216 1842, '44 "   "   Bank of Montreal, uncirculated, 2 pieces.
' 1217 1850, '2, '4, '7, Half Penny, Bank of Upper Canada, fine to uncirculated, 4 pieces.
" 1218 1858, '9, '76, One Cent, uncirculated, 3 pieces.
" 1219 1843, '54, One Penny Token, New Brunswick, fine, 2 pieces.
" 1220 1843, '54, Half Penny, New Brunswick, varieties, fine, 2 pieces.
2 1221 1861, '4, One Cent, New Brunswick, fine, 2 pieces.
50 1222 1861, Half Cent New Brunswick,   "
1 1223 1843, Penny and Half Penny Token, Nova Scotia, good, 2 pieces.
2 1224 1856 Penny and Half Penny Token, Nova Scotia, fine, 2 pieces.
4 1225 1861 Cent and Half Cent, Nova Scotia, uncirculated, 2 ps.
2 1226 1862 Cent, Nova Scotia, fine.
" 1227 1864 Cent and Half Cent, Nova Scotia, uncirculated, 2 pieces.
1 1228 1814 "Broke Token," Halifax N. S. very fine, scarce.
8 1229 1814 Half Penny Token, "Hosterman and Etter" Halifax, good, scarce.
" 1230 1814 Half Penny Token, Garrit and Alford, Halifax, good.
6 1231 1815 Half Penny Token, John Alex. Barry, Halifax, very fine, scarce.
5 1232 1815 Half Penny Token, Hosterman and Etter, Halifax, fine.
6 1233 1815 Half Penny Token, Starr and Shanon, Halifax, fine, scarce.
1 1234 1815 Half penny Token, Miles W. White, Halifax, fine, scarce.
2 1235 1816 Small Token obverse bank, reverse hardware. Halifax, scarce.
1 1236 1823 Half Penny Token, (Thistle) N. S. fine.
" 1237 1824 Penny and Half Penny Token, (Thistle) N. S. good, 2 pieces.

/ 1238   1832 Penny and Half Penny Token, (Thistle,) N. S.
         fine, 2 pieces.

21239   1840 Penny and Half Penny Token, (Thistle,) N. S.
         good to fine, 2 pieces.

" 1240   1813, 14, 15, 38, Trade and Navigation Penny Tokens,
         fine, 4 pieces.

" 1241   1812 Trade and Navigation Half Penny Tokens, varie-
         ties, good to fine, 3 pieces.

" 1242   1813 Trade and Navigation Half Penny Tokens, varie-
         ties, fine, 2 pieces.

/ 1243   1813, 14 Half Penny Token; reverse, Britania, good,
         2 pieces.

/ 1244   1813 Farthing, Trade and Navigation, good, scarce.

/ 1245   1813 Half Penny Token, Trade and Navigation, un-
         circulated, scarce.

£1246   1814, 15, 25 Wellington Half Penny Token, good to
         fine, 6 pieces.

6 1247   Farthing Token, obverse, Bust; reverse, Commercial
         Change, good, scarce.

2 1248   Obverse, male figure with shillalah; reverse, "Pure cop-
         per, &c.," fine, scarce.

" 1249   Small Tokens, "Speed the plow," fine, 2 pieces.

3£5 1250   One Farthing, W. L. White, Halifax, brass, fine.

/ 1251   Un Sou, Treason Token, Montreal, fine, rare.

" 1252   Belleville Butchers' Token, fine, scarce.

2/ 1253   Collection of the Un Sou series of Montreal, comprising
         different varieties, in good to fine condition, 24 pieces.

4/ 1254   Lot of large and small Coins and Tokens, copper and
         brass, fair to fine, 21 pieces.

WASHINGTON PIECES.

2£ 1255   Obverse, Bust, reverse, "Success to the U. S.," brass,
         good.

3£ 1256   Double head cent, copper, fine, scarce.

£ 1257   1783 One cent, "Unity States," brass, fine.

<> 1258   1783 Laureated Bust, reverse, Liberty seated, copper,
         very good.

1259   1783 Milt. Bust; reverse, same as last, copper, good.

/ 1260   1791 Small Eagle Cent, copper, good, rare.

1261   1791 Large   "   "   "   fine,   "

1262   1792 Half Dollar in copper. Obverse, Military bust,
         legend, "G. Washington. President 1, 1792"; re-
         verse, large spread eagle, group of 15 stars, legend,
         "United States of America," fine, excessively rare.

14 ¼5 1263 1792 Silver Half Disme. Obverse, bust of Martha Washington, legend, "*Lib. Par. of Science and Industry*, 1792," reverse, Eagle, legend, "United States of America," large planchet, obverse, fine, reverse, good, excessively rare.

2 ∞ 1264 1792 Same as last, but smaller planchet, pierced at top. Obverse, good, reverse, poor.

1 ♂ 1265 1792 Idler's copy of Wash. ½ dol. in copper, good.

5 1266 1792 Same, reverse, Idler's card, copper, proof.

75 1267 Liberty and Security Penny, large, thick, lettered edge, copper, fine, scarce.

55 1268 Brass Button, G. W. surrounded by an endless chain of 13 links containing initials of States, fine, rare.

13 1269 1792 Naked Bust, fine electrotype.

6 1270 1792 Cent, reverse, 13 stars over spread eagle, copy, fine.

MEDAL IMPRESSIONS, &C.

10 1271 1848 Large copper shell, obverse, represents two male figures one in the act of rescuing the other from a wreck, fine, size 56.

7 1272 1866 Copper shells, obverse and reverse, of the medal given by Congress, for the rescue of the passengers from the Steamer, San Fransisco, size 50, 2 pieces.

8 1273 1870 Copper shells, (obverse and reverse,) Cincinnati Industrial Exposition, proof, size 40, 2 pieces.

10 1274 1870 Copper shells, (obverse and reverse,) Bust of Suydam, National Academy of Design, N. Y., proof, size 40, 2 pieces.

6 1275 1865 Copper shells, (obverse and reverse,) Sanitary Fair, Chicago, proof, size 36, 2 pieces.

10 1276 1776 Copper shell, obverse, Peace and Commerce, American medal, "IV Jul. MDCCLXXVI," fine, size 40.

10 1277 Copper shell, naked bust of Henry Clay, 2½ by 1½ in., very fine.

12 1278 Bronze shell, bust of Garibaldi, very fine, size 26.

5 1279 Same, bust of Victor Emanuel, "   "   "

" 1280 Same, bust of Count De Cavour, very fine, size 26.

" 1281 French copper shell, bust of Josephine, fine, size 38.

9 1282 1876 Composition Medal, commemoration of the 100th Anniversary of Independence, fine, size 34.

10 1283 Medal in wood, Main Building, Centennial, very fine, size 48.

10 1284 Same, Art Gallery, fine, size 18.
7 1285 Same, Centennial, Washington, born, died, &c., fine, size 40.
" 1286 Same, bust of Albert T. Goshorn, fine, size 40.
" 1287 Same, General Hawley, fine, size 40.
15 1288 Same, Independence Hall, fine, size 40.
" 1289 Copper shell, silvered, containing the Declaration of Independence, and fac. similie signatures of the signers. View of the signing of the Declaration in the centre, very fine, size 7½ in. square.

U. S. FRACTIONAL CURRENCY.

80 1290 50, 25, 5 cents Postage Currency, 50 cents, slightly used, others clean, 3 pieces.
50 1291 50 cents, Head of Spinner, slightly creased.
75 1292 50   "   "   " Crawford, clean.
60 1293 50   "   "   " Dexter,   "
25 1294 25   "   "   " Washington, "
" 1295 25   "   "   " Walker,   "
10 1296 10   "   "   " Meredith, red seal, clean.
100 1297 50   "   "   " Washington, gilt ring, 15 and 10 cts.,
lot   Head of Liberty, 10 and 3 cts. Head of Washington, all considerably circulated, 6 pieces.

SILVER COINS OF SOUTH AMERICA.
PORTUGAL AND BRAZIL.

90 1298 1856 Petrus II, 2000 Reis, fine.
75 1299 1865 Same, fine, pierced.
40 1300 1855 Same, 1000 Reis, good.
" 1301 1856 Same   "   "   "
" 1302 1857   "   fine.
" 1303 1865   "   "
" 1304 1866   "   uncirculated.
23 1305 1854   "   500 Reis, good.
31 1306 1857   "   "   "   fine.
30 1307 1858   "   "   "   "
23 1308 1860   "   "   "   uncirculated.
" 1309 1861   "   "   "   "
" 1310 1865   "   "   "   good.
" 1311 1867   "   "   "   very fine.
10 1312 1854   "   200 Reis, fine.
" 1313 1862   "   "   "   good.
" 1314 1867   "   "   "   "

1868 Same   200 Reis, good.
1871 Large base coins, 200 and 100 Reis, fine, 2 pieces
1874 Same, 200 Reis, fine.

REPUBLIC OF BOLIVIA.

1831 "8 S," ($1.00) Military bust right, "Bolivar" on bust, good.
1835 Same, good.
1836 Same, fine.
1837 Same, good.
1844 Same, naked bust, "Bolivar" under bust, very, good, scarce.
1830 "4 S," (50 cts.) Military bust right, "Bolivar" on bust, fair.
1834 Same, naked bust, left, "Bolivar" on bust, scarce.
1830 "2 S." and "1 S." (25 and 12½ cts., bust right, same as last, good, 2 pieces.
1830 "½ S." (6¼ cts.) Same, uncirculated.

NEW GRANADA AND BOGOTA.

1834 "8 Reals" ($1.00,) Republic of Colombia, fine, scarce.
1839 "8 Dineros," Republic of New Granada, good, scarce.
1847 Same, Republic of New Granada and Bolivia, varieties, fine, 2 pieces.
1857 "One Peso," ($1.) good.
1860 Confederation "One Peso," good, scarce.
1869 "One Peso." United States of Colombia, fine, scarce.
1819 "2 Reals," New Granada, good.
1821 "   " Republic of Colombia, good.
1842 Same, fine.
1850, '2 Same, good, 2 pieces.
1867 "2 Decimos," U. S. of Colombia, pierced.
1840, 4, 7 One Real, New Granada, good, 3 pieces.
1853, 7 One Real, New Granada, varieties, 3 pieces.
Very small coins, various, good, 4 pieces.

REPUBLIC OF CHILI.

1848 "8 Reals," reverse, Eagle breaking a chain, good, scarce.

79 1342   1868 "One Peso," fine.
78 1343   1875 Same, fine.
15 1344   1857 "20 Cent," fine.
"   1345   1861 Same, fine.
10 1346   1866   "   "
7 1347   1856, 7 "One Decimo," good, 2 pieces.
, 1348   1865, 71, 74 Same, Fine, 3 pieces.
5 1349   Media Decimo, varieties, good, 5 pieces.
"   1350   1871 Two and One Centavos, nickel, 2 pieces.

MEXICO.

81 1351   1822 "8 Real" reverse small spread Eagle on cactus plant, good, scarce.
105 1352   1866 "One Peso" Maximillian, city of Mexico very fine, scarce.
90 1353   1866   "   "   "   Potosi Mint, very fine,
*." 1354   1867   "   "   "   City of Mexico, very good scarce.
" 1355   1866 (50 c) Maximillian, City of Mexico, fine, rare.
25 1356   1864 (10 c piece) "   (Mexico) very good, scarce.
15 1357   1865   "   "   "   (Zacaticas Mint) good, rare.
22 1358   1866   "   "   "   (Mexico) good, rare.
15 1359   1864 (5 c   ")   "   (M. mint) "   scarce.
21 1360   1865   "   "   "   (G.   "   "   rare.
" 1361   1866   "   "   "   "   "   "   "
7 1362   1822, 32 One Real good, 2 pieces.
6 1363   1862 "1 Real" Republic proof, rare.
5 1364   1823, "6 Medio Real," Empire, good, 2 pieces.
2½ 1365   1870, 2, 4, 5, "5 Centavos" Fine to uncirculated, 4 pieces.
4 1366   "¼ Reals" various, good to Fine, 9 pieces.

REPUBLIC OF PERU.

10 1367   1857 "2 Reals," good.
10 1368   1858 (50 cts.) "
35 1369   1859 Same.   "
13 1370   1828, 30, 38, "2 Reals " varieties, good, 3 pieces.
15 1371   1866 (20 cts.) Fine.
8 1372   One Real, 3 pieces, various, good.
" 1373   1864, 5, 6, 75, (10 ct. pieces,) Fine, 4 pieces.
4 1374   5 ct. pieces, good to Fine, 4 pieces.
2 1375   ¼ Reals, "Lima," various, good, 3 pieces.

MISCELLANEOUS SILVER COINS OF SOUTH AND CENTRAL AMERICA.

1376 1874 "4 Reals," U. S. of Venezuela, Fine.
1377 1874 Same, "One Real," Fine.
1378 1813 "8 Reals," Chihuahaw, bow and arrow, very rude, Fine, rare.
1379 1867 "One Peso," Guatemala, good.
1380 1866 (50 cts.) Republic of Costa Rica, good scarce.
1381 1864 (25 cts.)   "   "   "   "   "   "
1382 1865 (10 cts.)   "   "   "   "   fair.
1383 1865 (5 c. pieces,) fair to good, 2 pieces.
1384 1842 (1 Real.) Republic of Costa Rica, fair.
1385 1797 Spanish quarter having the die impression of a Costa Rica Coin on each side, a curiosity, fair, unique.

CONFEDERATE BONDS, &C.

1386 1863 March 2, $1000.00 Richmond, 8 coupons attached signed, scarce.
1387 1863 March 2, $1000.00 Richmond, with all coupons attached and signed, rare.
1388 1864 March 2, $1000.00 Cotton Bond, Richmond, with all the coupons attached and signed, rare.
1389 1863 March 2, $100.00, Richmond, all coupons attached and signed, pink paper.
1390 1863 Same, 8 coupons attached and signed, white paper
1391 1863   " all   "   "   "   "   pink   "
1392 1863   " unsigned, white paper.
1393 1863   " 8 coupons attached and signed.
1394 1863   "
1395 1863   " all coupons attached and signed, pink paper.
1396 $100.00 6 per ct., "None Taxable Certificate," unsigned
1397 1864 February 17, $500.00 note, Richmond, clean, scarce.
1398 1862 July 22, $100.00 "Interest Bearing Note," Richmond, clean.
1399 1862 August 28, same.
1400 1862 September 18, same.

THIRD DAY'S SALE.

MISCELLANEOUS COINS, MEDALS, &C.

1401 1770 Relief Church Token, Anderston, England, oval, lead, Fine, 2 pieces.

1402 Tyson & Co., Transfer Omnibus Ticket, brass, Fine, scarce.

1403 Calender Tokens, large and small, brass, Fine, 4 pieces.

1404 Eng. Model Penny, copper, brass centre, good, scarce.

1405 Same, White composition centre, very Fine, scarce.

1406 Copies of various U. S. pieces, copper, lead and brass, poor to Fine, 21 pieces.

1407 1865 Lincoln Medalet, "His memory is Enshrined in every Heart," copper, good, pierced, rare. Size 13.

1408 Lincoln Medalet, size of bronze cent, nickel, copper, brass, varieties, good to Fine, 9 pieces.

1409 1860 Cogan's Cards, "48 No. 10th St." copper, brass and white metal, silvered, tarnished, proofs size 13, 3 pieces, scarce.

1410 1783 Washington Cents. "Unity States," brass, poor to fair, 4 pieces.

1411 London Elephant Penny, electrotype.

1412 1797 English Two Penny Piece, copper, good, scarce.

1413 1803 Kettle Money, Half Eagle, brass, good.

1414 Idler's Lord Baltimore Penny, nickel, Fine.

1415 Clay, Taylor & Harrison Medalets, varieties, pierced, good, 6 pieces.

1416 Dickeson's N. C. Token, brass, Fine, scarce.

1417 1567 Copper Coin of Brunswick, nude female figure, Fine, rare.

1418 1549 Coin of Portugal, curious, Fine, rare.

1419 1600, Busts of Albert and Isabella, reverse, hands clasped around 3 heads of wheat, Fine and curious.

1420 1751 Small copper coin of Brunswick, Fine.

1421 Rude copper coins of Carthegenia, large and small, fair, 2 pieces.

1422 Curious early French Coins, brass, fair, 3 pieces.

1423 1797 "Five Baiocca," Rome, brass, good.

1424 Early and curious coins of Holland, large and small, copper, good, 3 pieces.

1425 1600 Copper Medalet, poor, odd and interesting.

1426 Spanish and German coins, old and curious, copper and brass, fair, 5 pieces.

1841 "States of Jersey $\frac{1}{12}$ and $\frac{1}{26}$" of a Shilling, copper, Fine, 2 pieces, scarce.
1844 Same, good, 2 pieces.
1858 Same, Fine, 2 pieces.
1851 Same, $\frac{1}{26}$ of a Shilling, Fine.
1834 Isle of Guernsey, 8 Doubles, uncirculated, scarce.
1818 Spanish dollar, silvered, covered on both sides with Chinese trade marks.
Two Spanish and one Mexican dollar, base metal, poor, 3 pieces.
Oval Omnibus Card, 6th and 8th Street Line, Phila., brass, good, scarce.
Same, Citizen's Line, German silver, good, scarce.
Same, Octagon Accomodation Line, good, scarce.
1837 Same, round, new line Roxbury Coaches, German silver, Fine, rare.
1858 Reed Street Ferry Ticket, Navy Yard route, Phila., copper, oval, good, rare.
Same, brass, pierced, poor.
1837 One Cent, Feuchtwanger's Composition, Fine.
1837 Baker's Soda Water Card, Charleston, S. C., German silver, fair, rare.
1866 "Price's Bros., Balt." Oyster card, German silver, good, scarce.
1872 "U. S. Mf'g. Co.," (Stencils,) Balt., German silver, Very Fine.
Col. Fisk, "Chicago Relief," Medalet, copper, pierced, Fine, scarce.
$\frac{1}{4}$ of a Spanish "Cob Dollar," value 25 cents.
Same, countermarked.
German silver card, "S. Goetz, Gallipolis, O." (5 cents.) Fine, scarce.
Brass Store Card, "G. Sauer," Richmond, Va.) brass, rare.
Same, C. Crooke & Co., Baltimore, "Pine Hill Coal," Fine, rare.
1863 Same, Shakspeare Club, Baltimore, (5 cts.) Fine, scarce.
Same, "Social Dem. T. Union," Baltimore, Fine, scarce.
Same, R. G. Potter, Baltimore, brass, good, scarce.
1860 "No Submission to the North," Medalet, brass, Fine, size 14, scarce.
Lincoln and Johnson, Medalet, copper, Fine.
1868 Seymour and Blair, photo. badge, Fine.

1456 Small collection of Medals. Medalets, Tokens, Cards,
      Engraved pieces, Coins, &c., brass, copper and white
      metal, poor to good. varieties, 31 pieces.

UNITED STATES CENTS.
(CONTINUED.)

1457 1823 over '22, very good. scarce.
1458 1823 Perfect date,   "   "
1459 1824 over '23, Good.
1460 1824 Perfect, close date. Fine.
1461 1824   "   broad "   "
1462 1825 Close date, Uncirculated. partly red. rare.
1463 1825 Broad "   Fine.
1464 1826 Sharp stars, "
1465 1826 Dull   "   "
1466 1827 Perfect die, uncirculated, partly red, scarce.
1467 1827 Cracked "   "   "   "   "
1468 1827 Fine, good color.
1469 1828 8 above the line, uncirculated, light olive.
1470 1828 8 on the line, Fine.
1471 1828 Large date, very Fine, red.
1472 1828 Small "   good.
1473 1829 Large "   Fine.
1474 1829 Small "   "
1475 1830 Uncirculated,
1476 1830 Cracked die, Fine.
1477 1830 Close large date, Fine.
1478 1830 Narrow small date, Fine.
1479 1831 Fine.
1480 1831 Cracked die. Fine.
1481 1831 Connected stars, very good.
1482 1832 Large stars, Fine, red.
1483 1832 Small "   good.
1484 1833 Cracked die, uncirculated, light olive.
1485 1833 Perfect die, Fine, steel color.
1486 1834 Large stars, Fine, light olive.
1487 1834 Small "   " dark.
1488 1834 Double portrait, Fine.
1489 1834 Connected stars, Fine, red.
1490 1835 Without Mint mark, double portrait, light olive,
      Fine.
1491 1835 With Mint mark, good.
1492 1835 Large stars, Fine, red.
1493 1835 Small "   very good.
1494 1836 Without Mint mark, uncirculated, light olive.

6	1495	1836 With Mint mark, very good.
"	1496	1837 With " " uncirculated, light olive.
"	1497	1837 Without " " Fine, light olive.
"	1498	1837 Cracked Die, Fine, been cleaned.
10	1499	1837 Beaded hair string, Fine.
	1500	1838 Uncirculated, red.
.	1501	1838 " light olive, very Fine.
	1502	1839 over '30 or '36 very good, rare.
1	1503	1839 " " " cracked die, good, rare.
1 10	1504	1839 '38 Head, uncirculated, light olive, scarce.
30	1505	1839 Silly Head, very good, scarce.
1 5	1506	1839 Booby " uncirculated, light olive, scarce.
56	1507	1839 '40 Head, uncirculated, partly red.
9	1508	1840 Small date. Fine.
1	1509	1840 Very good.
8	1510	1841 Perfect die, Fine.
5	1511	1841 Cracked die, "
90	1512	1842 Large date, uncirculated, light olive.
2	1513	1842 Small " Fine.
2	1514	1843 Date under Bust, very Fine, light olive.
22	1515	1843 " to left of Bust, Fine, dark steel color.
1	1516	1844 Uncirculated, red, (varnished.)
1	1517	1842 Liberty Head on each side, good, (soldered.)
40	1518	1845 Uncirculated, red.
5	1519	1846 6 on line, uncirculated, light olive.
22	1520	1846 6 below line, Fine.
"	1521	1847 Uncirculated, partly red.
80	1522	1848 " red.
20	1523	1849 " partly red.
5	1524	1850 " red.
15	1525	1850 " light olive.
16	1526	1851 " red.
15	1527	1851 " light olive.
5	1528	1852 " red.
15	1529	1852 " light olive.
"	1530	1853 " red.
"	1531	1853 " light olive.
"	1532	1854 " red.
22	1533	1854 " light olive.
40	1534	1855 Straight date, uncirculated, red.
6	1535	1855 Slanting " " "
22	1536	1855 Straight " " light olive.
"	1537	1855 Slanting " " " "
25	1538	1856 Uncirculated, red.
"	1539	1856 " light olive.

1540   1857 Large date, uncirculated, red.
1541   1857   "   "   "   light olive.
1542   1857 Small   "   "   red.
1543   1857   "   "   "   light olive.

CONFEDERATE PAPER MONEY.

1543½   1864 February 17, $1.00, Richmond, Head of Meminger, clean, 25 pieces.

1544   1864 February 17, $2.00, Richmond, clean, 25 pieces.

1545   1864 February 17, $5.00, Richmond, Head of Davis, clean, 25 pieces.

1546   1864 February 17, $20.00, Richmond, Head of Stephens, clean, 25 pieces.

1547   1864 February 17, $50.00, Richmond, Head of Davis, clean, 25 pieces.

1548   1864 February 17, $100.00, Richmond, Head of Mrs. Davis, clean, 25 pieces.

1549   1862 June, July, August and October, Richmond, (Train of Cars,) clean, (Interest Notes,) 6 pieces, scarce.

1550   1863 January, September, November and December, Richmond, (Negroes working in the field,) clean, (Interest bearing notes,) 4 pieces.

1551   1861 September 2, $5.00, Richmond, white paper, green and black ink, Head of Davis, clean, rare, 2 pieces.

1552   1861 September 2, $5.00, white paper, black ink, Head of Davis, clean, rare.

1553   1862 December 2, $5.00, Richmond, pink paper, (Capitol Building,) Head of Davis, back of the notes have 5s on a dark blue ground, clean, rare, 2 pieces.

1554   1863 April 6, Richmond, white paper, same Vignettes backs have on light blue ground, scarce, 4 pieces.

1555   1861 September 2, $5.00, Richmond, (female figure, seated on bale of cotton,) clean, scarce, 6 pieces.

1556   1861 September 2, $2.00, Richmond, clean, scarce, 2 pieces.

1557   1862 June 2, $2.00, Richmond, with green letters and numeral on face, scarce, 3 pieces.

1558   1862 June 2, $2.00, without green letters and numeral somewhat circulated, but perfect, 17 pieces.

1559   1863 December 2, Richmond, pink paper, clean, scarce.

1560   1863 April 6, Richmond, pink paper, clean, scarce.

1561   1862 June 2, $1.00, Richmond, (Steamship,) green letters and numeral on faces, clean, scarce, 2 pieces.

1562 1862 June 2, $1.00, without green letters and numeral on face, slightly soiled, 6 pieces.
1563 1864 February 17, 50 cts., Richmond, Head of Davis, (small notes,) new and clean, 5 pieces.
1564 1864 Same, slightly soiled, 6 pieces.
1565 1863 April 6, same, new and clean, 3 pieces.
1566 1863 Same, soiled, 6 pieces.
1567 1863 Set of C. S. A. notes, $100.00 (Interest bearing,) $100.00, $50.00, $20.00, $10.00, $5.00, $2.00, $1.00, new and clean, 8 pieces.
1568 1863, '4 Same, varieties in color of paper.
1569 1863, '4   "   "   "   "   "   "
1570 1863, '4   "   "   "   "   "   "
1571 1863, '4   "   "   "   "   "   "
1572 1863, '4   "   "   "   "   "   "
1573 1863, '4   "   "   "   "   "   "

UNITED STATES QUARTER DOLLARS.

1574 1796 Uncirculated, sharp, bright, beautiful impression, but unfortunately has been pierced and plugged at top, proof surface, rare.
1575 1804 Very good impression, scarce.
1576 1805 Very good.
1577 1805 Cracked die, good.
1578 1805 25 under the arrows on reverse, good.
1579 1805 Double letters and figures, very poor.
1580 1806 25 partly on arrows, reverse, very good.
1581 1806 25 distant from arrows, very good.
1582 1806 Cracked die, good.
1583 1806 over '5, good, scarce.
1584 1806 Same, cracked die, fine.
1585 1807 25 touches eagle's tail feathers on reverse, fine.
1586 1807 25 covered by arrows, good.
1587 1815 Nearly fine, very scarce.
1588 1815 Cracked die, fair.
1589 1818 Perfect die, uncirculated.
1590 1818 Cracked die,   "
1591 1818 Date separated, (1-81-8,) good, scarce.
1592 1819 Small date, fine.
1593 1820 Large   "   "
1594 1820 Small   " very good.
1595 1821 Large   " fine.
1596 1821 Small   " good.
1597 1822 Very good.

1598	1824	Fine.
1599	1825	Good.
1600	1825 over '24, fine.	
1601	1828 Large date, very good.	
1602	1828 Small " " "	
1603	1828 Large 25, " "	
1604	1831 Small 25, uncirculated.	
1605	1831 Large 25, "	
1606	1831 " letters, fine.	
1607	1831 Small " "	
1608	1832 Cracked die, good.	
1609	1832 Perfect die, fine.	
1610	1833 Fine.	
1611	1834 Without period at date, uncirculated, proof surface.	
1612	1834 Proof.	
1613	1831 Cracked die, uncirculated.	
1614	1835 " " "	
1615	1835 Perfect " "	
1616	1836 Date far from bust, uncirculated.	
1617	1836 " close to " fine,	
1618	1837 5 high up on reverse, very good.	
1619	1837 5 in proper place, very good.	
1620	1838 Drape bust, good.	
1621	1838 Liberty seated, uncirculated.	
1622	1839 Good.	
1623	1840 Fine.	
1624	1840 O. Mint, fine.	
1625	1841 " " good.	
1626	1841 Good.	
1627	1842 Fine.	
1628	1842 O. Mint, good.	
1629	1843 " " "	
1630	1843 Good.	
1631	1844 O. Mint, uncirculated.	
1632	1844 Fine.	
1633	1845 Uncirculated.	
1634	1846 Fine.	
1635	1847 Date close to bust, fine.	
1636	1847 " apart from bust, fine.	
1637	1848 Good.	
1638	1849 Good.	
1639	1850 Uncirculated.	
1640	1850 O. Mint, good.	
1641	1851 Good.	

1642 1852 Fine, scarce,
1643 1852 O. Mint, good, scarce.
1644 1853 Arrows, fine.
1645 1853 Cracked die arrows, uncirculated.
1646 1853 No arrows, very, good.
1647 1854 Fine.
1648 1855 Uncirculated.
1649 1856 Very good.
1650 1857   "   "
1651 1858 Uncirculated, Proof surface, rare.
1652 1859 Uncirculated.
1653 1860   "
1654 1861   "
1655 1862   "
1656 1863 Fine.
1657 1864 Very good.
1658 1865   "   "
1659 1865 Cracked die, very good.
1660 1866 Uncirculated.
1661 1867 S. Mint, fine.
1662 1868 Uncirculated.
1663 1869 S. Mint, very good.
1664 1870 Proof, scarce.
1665 1871   "   "
1666 1872 Fine.
1667 1873 No arrows, good.
1668 1873 Arrows, uncirculated.
1669 1874 Uncirculated.
1670 1875   "
1671 1876   "
1672 1877   "
1673 1878 Proof, scarce.

SOUTHERN STATE AND LOCAL NOTES, &C.

1674 $100.00, State of Mississippi, Greenback, clean,
1675 1860 August 1, $50.00, Bank of Commerce, Newburn, N. C., torn.
1676 1858 August 4, $20.00, Mechanics Bank, Augusta, Ga., fair.
1677 1858 October 23, $20.00, Bank of Charleston, S. C. clean.
1678 1856 January 29, $10.00, Exchange Bank, Norfolk, Va., good, 2 pieces.

1679 $10 00, Bank of East Tennessee, Knoxville; Merchant's and Mechanic's Bank, Wheeling, W. Va.; Mechanic Bank, Augusta, Ga,; Bank of South Carolina; Bank of Clarendon, Fayetteville, N. C., fair to good. 8 pieces.

1680   1862 October 15, $10.00 Virginia Treasury note, new and clean, 2 pieces.

1681 $5.00, Mechanics' Bank, Augusta. Ga.; No. Western Bank, Ringold, Ga.; Bank of Whitfield, Dalton. Ga.: Mineral Bank, Cumberland, Md., clean, 8 pieces.

1682   Same, State of N. C., Raleigh: Bank of Clarendon, Fayetteville, N. C.; Bank of Richmond, Va.; Fairmount Bank, Va.; Bank of Howardville, Va., clean, 5 pieces.

1683   Same, Bank Pittsylvania. Va., clean, 6 pieces.

1684   1862 March 13, Same, Virginia Treasury Note, clean, 3 pieces.

1685   1863 $3.00, Farmers', Merchants' and Bullion Bank, Washington, D. C.; Bank of Tennessee, Bank of Chattanooga, Macon and Brunswick R. R., Bank of Whitefield, Dalton, Ga., clean, 6 pieces.

1686 $3.00, Small Notes, Bank, State of Ga., Savannah, Central Bank, Staunton, Va., new and clean, 2 pieces.

1687 $2. Bank of Whitfield, Dalton: Bank of Fulton, Atlanta, N. Western Bank Ringold, Mechanics Bank, Augusta, State of Georgia, Milledgeville (Ga) good 6 pieces.

1688   1861 April 18 $2, Richmond, Va. Corporation, red face, clean, scarce.

1689 $2 Exchange Bank, Murfreesboro: Bank of Chattanooga; Mississippi Cent. R. R. Co., Holly Springs, (Tenn). fair 3 notes.

1690 $2 Greensboro Mutual L. I. and Trust Co.; Bank State of N. C., good, 7 pieces.

1691 $2 Small notes. Bank of Commonwealth Richmond, Va.; Manassas R. R. Co.; Central Bank, Staunton Va.; clean 3 notes,

1692   1862 Oct, 21, $1 Virginia Treasury notes, Richmond, clean, 11 pieces.

1693   The same, slightly circulated. 18 pieces.

1694   Same,   "   "   26 pieces.

1695 $1 N. W. Bank Ringold; Union Bank, Augusta; Southern Bank; Bainbridge Bank, Dalton: Planters and Mec. Bank, (Ga,) fair, 4 pieces.

/ 1696 $1.00, Bank of Chattanooga, Tenn.; Bank of City of
Petersburg, Va.; County Shenandoah, Woodstock,
Va.; County of Amherst, good, 5 pieces.

" 1697 90 cts., City of Lynchburg, May 1, 1862. $1 50/100, Bank
of the Commonwealth, June 1, 1862, Richmond,
Va., clean, 2 pieces.

" 1698 1862, '3, 75 cts., State of South Carolina, State of
North Carolina, good, 2 pieces.

" 1699 75 cts., Prince Edward County, State of Virginia,
good, 3 pieces.

^ 1700 75 cts., City of Lynchburg and County of Shenandoah,
clean, 2 pieces.

" 1701 1862 75 cts., Corporation of Danville, and Co. of Monroe, clean, 2 pieces.

" 1702 1862 50 cts., State of S. C. and city of Charleston,
S. C., good, 2 pieces.

" 1703 1862 50 cts., Mechanics' Saving and Loan, Savannah;
Bank of Empire State, Rome; State of Georgia,
Milledgeville, Ga., fair, 3 pieces.

" 1704 1862 50 cts., State of N. C., large notes, (Ship,) clean, 3 ps.

" 1705 1861 October 1, 50 cts., State of N. C., very small
notes, fair, 3 pieces.

" 1706 1863 January 1, 50 cts., State of Alabama, Montgom-
ery, small note, good.

- 1707 1861 '2, 50c. Commercial Bank, Richmond; Augusta
Co., Staunton; Shenandoah Co.; Rockingham Co.;
Harrisonburg, State of Va.; Danville Ins. Co.; small
notes, (Va.) good, 6 pieces.

/ 1708 1861 '2, 50c. Rockingham Co.; Commercial Bank; Augusta Co.; (Va) good, 8 pieces.

/ 1709 1861 '2, 50c. Corporation of Richmond and Cor. of Winchester; Rockingham Co.; Northumberland Co.; Prince
Edward Co. Rockbridge Co; Fluvanna Co (Va.) poor
to good, 8 pieces.

· 1710 1862 50c. Farmer's and Saving Bank; City of Lynchburg; Augusta Co.; City of Richmond, (Va.) fair to
good, 4 pieces.

1711 1863 May 11 40 cents, Shenandoah, Woodstock, Va.
clean, 4 pieces.

" 1712 1861 July 1, 25 cents, State of S. C.; ("Rooster note")
good, scarce.

" 1713 1862 May 25, 25 cents. Augusta Co.; 3 pieces.

" 1714 25 cent State of N. C., large and small, good, 3 pieces.

· 1715 1861 June 25c. Corporation of Winchester, Va. large
notes, good, 2 pieces.

/ 1716   1861 25c. Rockingham Co; Shenandoah, Co; Augusta
Co.; Bland Co.; Monroe Co.; Rockbridge Co.; Rap-
pahanock Co.; (Va.) large and small, fair to fine, 20
pieces.

" 1717   1861 '2, '3, 20 cents, Dumfries, Shenandoah Co.; (Va.)
large and small, fine 4 pieces.

" 1718   1861 '2, 20 c. Bank State of N. C., and State of S. C.,
large and small, fair to good, 4 pieces.

" 1719   1862 '3, 15 cts. Augusta Co.; Mecklenburg Co.; Prince
Edward Co.; Craig Co.; Shenandoah Co., (Va.) good
10 pieces,

" 1720   1862 Same City of Charleston, 3 cts. City of Lynchburg,
Va. State of S. C., poor to good, 3 pieces.

" 1721   1861 '2. 12½c. Shenandoah Co., and New Market, good
3 pieces.

" 1722   1861 10 cents State of N. C., Raleigh, good, 3 pieces.

" 1723   1862, '3, 10 cts, State of N. C., varieties, clean, 3 pieces.

" 1724   1861 10 cts. City Council of Augusta, Ga ; and Bank of
the State of S. C., good, 2 pieces.

" 1725   1861, '2, 10 cts. Corporation of Shepherdstown; City of
Richmond; Pendleton Co.; city of Lynchburg; Corporation of Charlestown; Augusta Co.; Prince Edward Co.; New Market; Shenandoah Co.; Manassas
Gap. R. R. Co.; Rockingham Co., (Va) fair to fine,
14 pieces.

" 1726   1861 October 19, Same, Portsmouth Saving Fund
Society, good, 2 pieces.

" 1727   1862 December 20, 5 cts., New Market, Va., fine.

" 1728   1861, '3, 5 cts., State of N. C., large and small notes,
good, 4 pieces.

" 1729   1841 July 10, 5 cts., Farmers' and Mechanics' Bank,
of Frederick County, good, rare.

" 1730   1862, '3, 5 cts., New Market, Rockingham County,
Shenandoah County, good, 3 pieces.

AMERICAN COLONIAL COINS, &C.

/ 50 1731   1652 Pine Tree Shilling, large thin planchet, obverse
good, reverse poor, rare.

80 1732   1652 Pine Tree Shilling, same, cracked die, fair, rare.

- 30 1733   1652 Pine Tree Shilling, small thick planchet, very
good, rare.

// 1734   1652 Oak Tree Shilling, solid copper electrotype, silvered, very fine, scarce.

60 1735   1652 Oak Tree Sixpence, same as last, very fine, scarce.

6 1736   Lord Baltimore Penny, struck copy in copper, smaller and thinner than Idler's copy, fine, rare, size 13.

" 1737   same, Idler's copy in silver, dull proof, size 13¼.

" 1738   same, in brass, Idler's card erased, damaged proof.

*7^* 1739   "Mark Newby" Piece, or St. Patrick Half Pence, circulated in New Jersey, brass crown inserted near top, over the harp, copper, good, rare.

" 1740   Sommer Islands Shilling, struck copy in copper, proof, scarce.

1741   "U. S. A. Bar cent," solid, struck copy in copper, proof.

*v^* 1742   Carolina Elephant Penny, "*God Preserve Carolina And The Lords: Proprietors*, 1694." This piece has every appearance by age and color of being genuine, although we think it a cast. Sold as doubtful, copper, good.

25 1743   1721 "Colonies Francoises," or Louisiana copper, good, scarce.

1 1744   1722 same, electrotype, good.

25 1745   1722 "Wood Half Penny," fine.

5 1746   1723 same, large Planchet, good.

" 1747   1723 same, small Planchet, "

80 1748   1723 Wood Farthing, uncirculated, light olive, rare.

10 1749   Rosa Americana Penny, Rose variety, fair, scarce.

1 1750   same, Rose crowned, pierced, very poor.

65 1751   1722 Rosa Americana Half Penny, Rose variety, very fine, rare.

35 1752   1723 same, Rose crowned, fine, rare.

8 1753   1737 "Granby Copper," 3 hammers crowned, fine thin electrotype.

1 1754   1737 same, thick electrotype, good.

1 1755   same, Broadaxe variety, electrotype, fair.

*8^* 1756   1760 Voce Populi, broken die, letter P under bust, **fine**, scarce.

15 1757   1760 same, letter P in right field, different variety, both obverse and reverse; good, scarce.

" 1758   1760 same, without letter, good, scarce.

5 1759   1760 same, variety in letter, pierced, otherwise good, scarce.

80 1760   1767 "Colonies Francoises," or La. Copper, without countermark, fine, rare.

40 1761   1767 same with countermark (R. F.) fine, scarce.

62 1762   1773 Virginia Cent, large planchet, obverse good, reverse fine, scarce.

11 1763 1773 same, small planchet.
50 1764 1766 Pitt Token, electrotype, good.
5 1765 1778 " Non. Depen. Dens Status," electrotype, good.
62 1766 1778 Rhode Island Piece, obverse Ship, reverse ships, island, boats, &c., brass, very fine, rare.
15 1767 1776 Continental Currency (Dickeson's) white metal, proof, size 24.
27 1768 1781 North American Token, copper, fine.
6 1769 1785 Confederatio Piece, fine electrotype copy.
15 1770 1783 Nova Constellatio Piece, "U. S. 1000," silver plated copy, very fine, scarce.
" 1771 1783 Same, "U. S. 500," silver plated copy, very fine, scarce,
28 1772 "Georgius Triumpho," "Voce Populi, 1783," copper, good, scarce.
35 1773 1783 Chalmers Annapolis Shilling, (copy,) copper, silvered, fine.
110 1774 Carolina Piece, ship, reverse, shield and stars, fine, scarce.
-- 1775 Columbia Token, obverse, Bust "Columbia," in large letters over Bust, reverse, figure of Justice, copper, fine, scarce,
1776 same, "Columbia" in small letters over bust, copper, fine, scarce.
30 1777 same, "Columbia," under bust, fine, scarce.
35 1778 same, Large bust, without the word "Columbia, fine, scarce.
25 1779 1787 Nova Eborac, or N. Y. Cent, fair, date plain, scarce.
15 1780 same, good, date plain.
1 1781 same, poor, date undiscernable,
215 1782 1787 "Immunis Columbia," an excellent specimen, almost fine, copper, rare.
1 1783 Electrotype copy of the same, good.
5 1784 1787 "Neo. Eboracus, Excelsior," fine electrotype.
" 1785 1787 "Excelsior" piece, Arms of N. Y., electrotype, fine.
30 1786 1787 " Geo. Clinton" piece, struck copy in copper, very fine, scarce.
61 1787 1787 Franklin or Fugio Cent, "States United," very fine, light olive, scarce.
1 1788 1786 same, "United States" variety, good, scarce.
" 1789 1787 same, struck copy, copper, uncirculated.
" 1790 1787 Mass. Cent, broken planchet, very good.
1 1791 1787 same, perfect planchet, good.

16 1792 1788 same, broken planchet, fine.
" 1793 1788 same, perfect " very good.
99 1794 1787 Mass. Half Cent, very good, rare.
5 1795 1787 same, Electrotype, good.
16.30 1796 1690 "Baltimore Town Piece", or "Barry Standish Three Pence", obverse, bust of Standish, around which are the words, "*Baltimore Town, July* 1, '90", reverse, "*Three Pence*" in two lines, in centre, (between two parallel bars or dashes,) around this the name "*Barry Standish*", the letters of which are interlaced by an endless chain of small beads; reeded edge, very fine, in fact no marks of circulation can be distinguished, but a little weakly struck in centre. It is evident from a hair line extending across field of reverse, that the die cracked, and to this fact may be attributed the remarkable rarity of this desirable coin. Silver, size of half dime.
15 1797 1794 Talbot Allum and Lee, N. Y. Cent, fine, slightly corroded, scarce.
" 1798 1794 same, very good, scarce.
30 1799 Kentucky Cent, thick planchet, lettered edge, uncirculated, light olive, rare.
160 1800 Kentucky Cent, thin planchet, plain edge, uncirculated light olive, rare.
*1801 1796 Kentucky Token, "P. P. P. Mydleton," fine electrotype.
*1802 1796 Castorland Half Dollar, electrotype, silvered, uncirculated.

(A large variety of Colonial Coins will be found in Part II of this sale, to be sold October 19, 20, 21.)

FOREIGN BRASS MEDALS, MEDALETS, &C.

76 1803 1588 Fleet of vessels, reverse, a castle, in the sea, old and curious German Medal, fine, size 32.
85 1804 Obverse map of a city and its defences, reverse Latin inscription, nine lines, old and curious, fine, size 32.
77 1805 Male and female figures embracing; city in the distance; reverse, two dogs attacking a lion; probably a German medal, old and curious, fine size 31.
52 1806 1688 Religious Medal, Bust in canonicals; reverse 7 medalion busts of different Bishops, broken at the top, otherwise good, size 31.
65 1807 1593 Bust of Henry IV of France; reverse, swords crowned, very good, size 26.

// 1808   Equestrian figure, Duke of Cumberland, reverse, soldiers, &c., very poor, old and rusty, size 26.

6 1809   1744 Obverse, female figure with child in her lap, reverse 4 military figures, with maps spread out before them, good, size 27.

/21810   Obverse bust of Admiral Capt, and General Stadhoulder, reverse heraldry, &c, pierced, poor, size 26.

" 1811   1757 Bust of Frederick, Prussia, reverse, female figures, cannon &c, fine, size 31.

" 1812   Bust of Louis XV of France, reverse, male and female figures, representing France and England, very fine, size 26.

/5 1813   1870 Bust of Beethoven, reverse, lyre, scroll, laurel wreath &c, very thick, very fine, and artistic, size 24.

26 1814   Bust of Napoleon by Andrieu, reverse, inscription in nine lines, "Born, Died," &c., very fine and artistic, size 20.

7 1815   Bust of Herr Alexander, (Magician,) reverse, Presented, &c., N. Y. 1847, thick and very fine, size 18.

" 1816   1848 Frederic William IV, reverse, wreath, cross, &c., ring attached, fine, size 19.

" 1817   1853 Bust of Napoleon, reverse, tomb of Napoleon, varieties, fine, 2 pieces, size 15.

" 1818   Obverse, bust of Caroline, Queen Consort of England, Medalet, fine, size 18.

" 1819   Busts of William and Adelaide, reverse, crown, wreath, &c., fair, size 16.

" 1820   Obverse, Bust of Hih, reverse, "To Commemorate the Visit of Hih, the Shah of Persia," June, '73, fine, size 16.

" 1821   1869 Bust of Pius IX, reverse, a Church, fine, size 16

AMERICAN POLITICAL BRASS MEDALETS.

2 1822   Bust of Jackson, "Andrew Jackson, President," reverse "Commemorating the Victories of Our Hero, &c." good, pierced, rare, size 18.

" 1823   1840 Bust of Maj. General W. H. Harrison, reverse, log cabin, "The People's Choice," fine, pierced, size 15.

" 1824   1840 same, variety on reverse, "The Choice of the People," good, pierced, size 15.

" 1825   same, "The Hero of Tippecanoe", good, pierced.

" 1826   same, good, pierced, size 18.

1827 1841 same, reverse, Eagle, "Go It Tip", "Come It Tyler", fine, pierced, size 16.

1828 same : reverse, eagle, "Tippecanoe", fine, pierced, size 15.

1829 1841 same; reverse, log cabin, "The People's Choice", fine, pierced.

1830 Bust of Henry Clay, "The Farmer of Ashland," reverse wreath, The Noble Patriotic Supporter Of The People's rights, good, pierced, size 15.

1831 Bust of General Scott, reverse, eagle, "Scott and Graham," very fine, pierced, size 18.

1832 same; variety in bust, reverse, a battle, "Sandy's Lane," "Scott Wounded," fine, very good, size 18.

1833 same ; variety in bust, reverse, Chippewa, &c., and seven lines, very fine, pierced, size 16.

1834 Bust of Freemont, "Free soil and Free speech," reverse eagle, &c., fine, size 18.

1835 same ; reverse, eagle on a globe, very fine, size 14.

1836 1848 Bust of Taylor, reverse, spinning wheel, sheep, &c., fair, pierced, size 18.

1837 1851 Bust of Chas. Sumner, reverse, eagle, "Civil Rights for All," good, pierced, scarce, size 15.

1838 Bust of Pierce, reverse, eagle, "Pierce and King," fine, pierced, size 17.

1839 same; variety in bust, reverse, "For President", &c., in 10 lines, pierced, very fine, size 16.

1840 Bust of Buchanan, reverse eagle, "31 states" good, pierced, size 18.

1841 Bust of John A. Bell, reverse eagle, good, size 18.

1842 same ; Variety on obverse, "The Constitution," pierced, fine, size 18.

1843 1860 Bust of Lincoln, reverse "Rail Splitter of The West," very fine, size 18.

1844 same; Variety in bust &c., reverse blank, good pierced, size 19.

1845 1864 same. Reverse O. K. in an endless chain, very fine, size 12.

1846 Bust of McClellan, reverse eagle, thick, very fine, size 15.

1847 1868 Bust of Grant facing, reverse, "I Propose To Fight It Out", &c., thick, very fine, pierced, size 18

1848 1868 same, thinner than last. fine, pierced, size 18.

1849 1868 Bust of Seymour and Blair, reverse, wreath, "General Amnesty", &c., proof, pierced, size 18.

1850 1872 Bust of Greely, "The Sage of Chappaqua," reverse, eagle, proof, pierced, with ring attached, size 15.

1851   same, without ring, good.
1852   1872 Obverse, bust of Grant, reverse. "Patient of Toil"
&c., thick, proof, size 16.
1853   1879 same; reverse, "Struck and Distributed in the
Municipal Parade," Phila., Dec., 16, 1879, proof,
size 16.
1854   Seymour and Blair, photo. badge, in brass frame, very
fine, size 18.
1855   same, Grant and Colfax.
1856   Various Political Medalets, large and small, fair to very
fine varieties, 10 pieces.

AMERICAN POLITICAL WHITE METAL
MEDALS, MEDALETS, &C.

1857   Bust of Henry Clay, reverse, Angel inscribing a monument, proof, scarce, size 28.
1858   Bust of Maj. Gen'l. Taylor, reverse. "I Ask No Favors"
&c., good, pierced, size 24.
1859   Bust of Harrison, reverse. Bunker Hill Monument,
poor, size 28.
1860   same, reverse, Log Cabin, good, size 24.
1861   Bust of Bell, reverse, bust of Everett, proof, size 20.
1862   Bust of Fremont "Jessie's Choice" rev. "Fremont and
Dayton" proof, size 18.
1863   1864 Bust of Lincoln "Honest Old Abe" "Union Candidates" &c., fine, pierced, size 22.
1864   same. "Wide Awakes" proof, size 12.
1865   Naked Bust of Johnson, "And. Johnson, 17th President
U. S." Proof, size 13.
1866   Nacked Bust of McClellan, rev. wreath, "Nec Querere,
Nec Spernere Honorem," thick, very fine, size 22.
1867   same. Reverse Eagle, shield, flag, &c., very fine, size 22.
1868   same. Reverse, "People's Choice" good, pierced, size 20.
1869   1864 same. Reverse. Head of Washington, good, pierced,
size 18.
1870   1868 Brass shell Medal of Grant. "*I Propose to
More Immediately on Your Works*," very fine, size 20.
1871   Bust of Grant, "I Intend to Fight It Out" &c., proof
size 21.
1872   same ; reverse, "Republican Candidate," &c., proof,
size 18.
1873   Busts of Grant and Colfax, reverse. Clasped hands, &c.,
proof, size 17.

1871 Busts of Seymour and Blair, reverse, "Nat. Dem. Candidates," &c., thick, proof, size 24.

1875 Bust of Seymour, facing, reverse, a star, "No North, No South", &c., proof, pierced, size 20.

1876 same, reverse, "Dem. Candidate," &c., proof, pierced, size 18.

1877 Bust of Grant, "Inaugurated President, March 4, 1869" proof, size 32.

1878 same, pierced, with ring.

1879 Bust of Greely, "For President," &c., proof, pierced, size 17.

1880 Bust of Hayes; Reverse, Bust of Wheeler, good, pierced, size 20.

1881 Same, proof, size 16.

1882 1870 Bust of Grant "In honor of The 15th Amendment," proof, size 18.

1883 Bust of Grant, "Philadelphia's Honored Guest," Dec. 16th, 1879.

MISCELLANEOUS AMERICAN WHITE METAL MEDALS, MEDALETS &C.

27 1884 1783 "Libertas Americana," Reverse. "Communi Consensu" very good, original, rare, size 28.

6 1885 1860 View of Capitol Building, Washington, shells, proof, size 32, 2 pieces.

" 1886 1865 A Fire Engine. Reverse. "In Peace Fireman," &c. (Phila. Oct. 16) dull proof, pierced, size 32

125 1887 1866 Goddess of Liberty, sailor, soldier, children, flags and eagle "G. A. R. 1861—1866" Reverse, eagle, shield, &c., beautiful and artistic proof, size 32.

16 1888 1869 March 4, Grant Inauguration Medal, proof, size 32.

10 1889 Masonic Temple, N. Y. "Dedicated June 2, 1875." shield shape, buckle attached, length 2½ in., very fine, scarce.

3 1890 1876 Medalion Bust of Washington, eagle, angels, &c., "International Exhibition, Phila." proof, pierced, size 34.

" 1891 Eagle surrounded by the words "U. S. Quarter Master's Dep't" reverse blank, good, pierced, size 28.

" 1892 1858 Atlantic Telegraph, 5 of Aug. Reverse. Bro. Jon. and Yankee, proof, size 20.

" 1893 1860 St'r. Great Eastern, Reverse. Arrived at N. Y. &c.," proof, size 20.

10 1894 Same, different Reverse, proof.

4 1895 Bombardment of F't. Sumter, Reverse, "Evacuation" &c., proof, size 22.

" 1896 1865 Bust Gen. Humphries, Reverse, trefoil; dull proof, pierced, size 20.

" 1897 1866 Shield, flags, &c., July 4. Reverse, "Arms of Pa." Gettesburg, Pa. Vol's July 3, 1863, proof, size 24.

" 1898 1869 Semi-Cent'l I. O. O. F. Phila. Bust of Tho's. Wildey fine, pierced, size 24.

' 1899 1871 Cin. Indus. Exhibition Building, Reverse. "Chamber of Commerce," very fine, size 16

4 ✗1900 1872 M'd, Ins. Building, Reverse, "25th Anniversary. Oct, '72", (Balt.) proof, thick, size 15.

22 1901 1874 Masonic Temple, reverse, emblems, Springfield. Mass. proof, size 18.

' 1902 1876 Fountains, reverse. Catholic. To. Ab-ti. Un. of Am. Fairmount Park, July 4, proof, size 24.

" 1903 Small Cent'l and other medalets, poor to good, 5 pieces.

LARGE FOREIGN COPPER COINS, &C.

-' 1904 1700 Isle of Man, eagle, Reverse, three legs; brass, fair. rare. .

12 1905 1733 Same, variety, fine, scarce.

10 1906 1733 Same. Good.

" 1907 1758 Crown and Monogram, Reverse, 3 legs ; fine, scarce.

" 1908 1763 Ship, Reverse, Crown and Monogram, Danish America, fair, scarce.

21 1909 1764 Same, large as English ½ penny, very fine, rare.

15 1910 1786 Isle of Man, Penny, Geo. III, 3 legs, fine, rare.

31 1911 1786 Same, Half Penny, good match to preceding.

3 1912 1788 Barbadoes Penny, Pineapple, fair.

7 1913 1788 Same, Cracked Die, fair.

85 1914 1791 Sierra Leone Penny, lion, clasped hands &c., proof, light olive, scarce.

" 1915 1791 Same, Half Penny, good match to preceding.

25 1916 1792 Barbadoes Penny, Neptune in chariot, good, scarce.

20 1917 1793 Bermuda Penny, ship, proof, rare.

1 1918 1783 Same, Ornamental cross on bust of Geo. III, good, rare.

10 1919 1798 Isle of Man Penny, Geo. III, 3 legs, good, pierced, scarce.

7 1920 1798 Same, Half Penny, fair.

11 1921 1806 Bahama " " ship, fine, scarce.

9 1922 1810 Gibraltar, 2 Quartos, good.

7 1923 1810 Same, Varieties, 2 and 1 Quarto, good, 2 pieces.

6/ 1924 1811 Isle of man, Bank Penny, 3 legs, poor.
" 1925 1811 Same Bank Half Penny, good.
7 1926 1813 Same, Penny, good.
4/ 1927 1813 Demerara Token, 1 Stiver, very fine, scarce.
4 1928 1813 Same, Half Stiver, uncirculated, scarce.
7 1929 1813 Gibraltar, 2 Quartos, good.
6/ 1930 1815 Magdalen Island Penny Token, seal, fair.
-8 1931 1815 Ceylon, 1 Stiver, Elephant, fine, scarce.
6 1932 1816 Caracas Coin (¼) good, scarce.
" 1933 1819 Italian Coin, "Tornesi," thick, good.
" 1934 1820 Gibraltar, 2 Quartos, poor.
" 1935 1821 St. Helena, Half Penny, fine, scarce.
" 1936 1829 1 Skilling, crossed arrows, good.
" 1937 1833 "Liberia, 1 cent", man, tree, &c., fine.
" 1938 1835 Republic of Chili 1 and ½ Centavo (star) thick, un-
         circulated, scarce, 2 pieces.
" 1939 1838 1 Stiver, "Trade and Navigation" good.
" 1940 1839 Isle of Man, Half Penny, 3 legs, good.
" 1941 1813 Venezuela, 1 Centavo, and Gibraltar, 2 quarts, fair,
         3 pieces.
/2 1942 1844 Republic of Uruguay, "40 Centesimos" (sun) very
         thick, fine, scarce.
8 1943 1846 New Foundland Token, very fine.
26 1944 1847 Liberia, 2 cents, (tree) fine, scarce.
32 1945 1847 Same, 1 cent, good.
6 1946 1848 New Grenada, "1 Decimo De Real," good.
" 1947 1851 Republic of Chili, 1 Centavo, large, thin, fine.
" 1948 1851 Same, Varieties 1 and ½ Centavo, good, 2 pieces.
/0 1949 1852 Venezuela, 1 Centavo, large, fine.
6 1950 1852 Same, Smaller, fine.
/2 1951 1853 Portugal, "½ Macuta" large, very fine,
" 1952 1853 Republic of Chili, 1 and ½ Centavo, fine, 2 pieces.
" 1953 1854 Argentine Confederation, 4 and 1 Centavo, fine,
         2 pieces.
" 1954 1855 7 Prince Edward Island Token, fine, 2 pieces.
7 1955 1857 Republic of Uruguay "40 Centesimos," thick, fine.
6 1956 1857 Same, "20 Centesimos," good.
7 1957 1857, '8, "Honduras Pieces" (8 p's,) mountains, tree,
         &c., fair, scarce, 2 pieces.
/2 1958 1858 New Zealand Penny Token, good.
6 1959 1858 Venezuela, 1 Centavo, fine.
/5 1960 1860 New Foundland Token, "Fishery Rights," fine.
26 1961 1862 Liberia, 2 cents, (tree) good, scarce.
/6 1962 1862 Same, 1 cent, fine, scarce.

1963   1862 Honduras (4 P's) mountains, castles, &c., good, scarce.
1964   1862 Same, (2 P's) fine, scarce.
1965   1862 Straits Settlements, 1 cent and ½ cent, good, scarce, 2 pieces.
1966   1862 Venezuela, 1 centavo, fine.
1967   1863 Same, good.
1968   1863 Sarawak, 1 cent, good, scarce.
1969   1865 New Foundland, one cent, fine.
1970   1867 Victor Eman'l II, 10 Centesimi, fine.
1971   1869 Republic of Uruguay (sun) 4, 2 and 1 Centesimos, (full set) uncirculated, 3 pieces.
1972   1870 Sarawack, 1 cent and ½ Cent, uncirculated, red, scarce, 2 pieces.
1973   1871 Prince Edward Island, 1 cent, Cracked Die, uncirculated, red, scarce.
1974   1871 Same, Perfect Die, fine.
1975   1872, '3, New Foundland, 1 cent, fine, 2 pieces.
1976   1873 Straits Settlements, 1, ½, and ¼ cent, uncirculated, red, 3 pieces.
1977   1874 Same, uncirculated, red, scarce.
1978   Japan, 2, 1 and ½ Sen. (full set) uncirculated, 3 pieces.
1979   Same, 1 rin. uncirculated.
1980   "Ships, Colonies and Commerce" English flag, uncirculated, red.
1981   J. Brown's Canada Token, ship, thistle, &c., fine, scarce.
1982   Uruguay, Venezuela, Peru, Straits Settlements, Belgium, good to fine, 7 pieces.
1983   Isle of Man, New Granada, Gibraltar, St. Helena, New foundland; coins and tokens, fair to good, 7 pieces.

SMALL FOREIGN COPPER COINS, &C..

1984   1678 Charles II, Scotch Farthing, fair, rare.
1985   1692 Same, variety.
1986   Queen Anna Farthing, fine, rare, variety.
1987   1782 9; Cayenne Colonies, 2 Sous, good, 2 pieces.
1988   1792 Farthing, John Howard, fine.
1989   1802 Ceylon, Elephant Coin, size of farthing, good, scarce.
1990   1804 Island of Sumatra (Arms) scarce, fine, 2 pieces.
1991   Same, "Rooster" Coins, fine, 2 pieces.
1992   1812 Cartagena, ½ Estado, rude, good, scarce.
1993   1844 '8 Dominica Republic. (¼) good, scarce, 2 pieces.
1994   1843 '4, '5, Belgium, 1 cent, very small, good, 3 pieces.

1995 1852 Austria, 5 Centesimi, varieties, good, 2 pieces.
1996 1859 '60 Danish West Indies, fine, 2 pieces.
1997 1863 Republic of Peru, 2 and 1 Centavos, nickel, fine, 2 pieces.
1998 1864 Same, fine, 2 pieces.
1999 1865 Costa Rica, 1 Centavo, nickel, good, scarce.
2000 1868 Danish West Indies, 1 cent, brass, fine, scarce.
2001 1878 Netherlands, 1 cent, fine, scarce.
2002 Germany and Austria. Collection of small coins, poor to good, varieties, 25 pieces.
2003 Frankfurt, collection of small coins, 1, 2, and 3 Heller, fair, to fine, varieties, 12 pieces.
2004 Germany, 3 Pfenning, varieties, 11 pieces.
2005 Same. 2 Pfenning, 12 pieces.
2006 Same, 1 " good to uncirculated, varieties, 12 pieces.
2007 South America, ½ and ¼ Centavo, small, good, 4 pieces.
2008 German and English Coins very small, varieties, fair to good, 15 pieces.
2009 Sweden and Norway, good, varieties, 6 pieces.
2010 Norway and Denmark, fine, varieties, 2 pieces.
2011 Denmark, 2 and 1 Ore, 1874, uncirculated, 2 pieces.
2012 Same, fine, 2 pieces.
2013 Sweden, 1 Ore, varieties, 9 pieces.
2014 Chas. II Scotch Coin, poor, rare.
2015 Swiss and German Coin, copper and base, small, varieties, fair to fine, 12 pieces.

ERRATUM.

Lot 1796 should read *Standish Barry Three Pence, bust of Barry.*

PRICED CATALOGUES

—OF—

The Smith Cabinet,

PART FIRST, 3 *Days Sale,* . $0.75

PART SECOND, 3 *Days Sale,* . . 0.75

Forwarded soon after Sales by

MASON & CO.

143 North Tenth Street, Philadelphia.